CLOUDBURST

Suzanne Cass

S C
STORM CLOUD
PRESS

To Alex and Gwyneth

CHAPTER ONE

Penny Smith fumbled with her car keys, juggling the large bunches of flowers, trying not to drop them as she maneuvered the key into the lock. She was late. It was after seven o'clock, and all the shops were closed. Thankfully, the florist had stayed open especially for her, so she could pick up the samples for Naomi. Now, she needed to get back to the ranch to help with the dinner rush.

Preparations were in full swing for Cat and Levi's wedding on Saturday, in four days' time: the first day of summer. Penny's mind swirled with the million and one things she still had left to do. As one of Cat's three bridesmaids, she had yet to try on her dress. It was still hanging on the hook on the back of her door. Stella's and Emily's dresses had fit them both perfectly. Penny just hadn't found the time yet. In typical Cat style, she'd chosen a simple, apple-green shift that came to just above the knee. Penny knew it'd look good against her blonde hair and pale skin. What color eye makeup should she wear? She'd have to ask Stella what—

"Those look heavy. Would you like a hand?" A voice came from somewhere behind her, across the deserted parking lot.

Penny froze.

That voice.

She knew that voice.

Would know it anywhere.

All the strength drained from her body and she felt limp, unable to move. Unable to turn around and face her tormentor. Unable to even breathe.

The flowers and her keys dropped from her numb fingers onto the black asphalt.

He'd found her.

What should she do? How should she react?

Her heart kicked like a mule in her chest and she drew in a sharp gasp, finally moving one foot and then the other until she turned to see him.

"Hi, honey. You're looking good." The man smiled at her. "Blonde suits you. I like your new style."

Penny moved her lips, but no sound came out.

Mitch stood around twenty yards away, in jeans and a soft sweater that stretched across his chest, designed to emphasize the chiseled pecs beneath. He was good-looking, in that boy-next-door type of way. Not overly tall, he was clean-shaven, with short and stylish, jet-black hair. She tried to read his mood, searched his eyes for some clue as to what he was thinking. But his dispassionate half-smile told her nothing. She knew that dark, controlling malignant side of him was still there, however. Lurking in the depths of his soul.

"I've missed you. You sure were hard to track down."

What had she done wrong? Where had she slipped up? How had he traced her?

Penny's gaze darted around the parking lot. It was at the rear of a set of shops, off the back of Main Street. And completely deserted. Everyone had locked up and left for the day, including the florist who'd zoomed off as soon as Penny was out the door. She was alone. She could hear cars going past on a secondary road in the distance, but had no hope they might see something was wrong.

Mitch walked toward her, and she gave a squeak of fright.

He bent down to retrieve the flowers. "These are pretty. Can I give you a hand to put them in your car? What are they for?" His eyes narrowed and Penny caught a flash of something she would recognize anywhere. There it was. The monster.

He'd taken her completely by surprise; knocked the breath out of her for a second. She needed to stop acting like a scared toddler. Get some backbone. Get rid of him.

"No, you can't," she said, making her voice as cold and controlled as possible. "You need to step away from me, Mitch. You're breaking the restraining order by being this close."

"Oh, honey. You don't need some stupid restraining order." He gave her a soft frown, full of anguish and hurt. But Penny wasn't fooled by that look.

"Here, let me help you," he said again, completely ignoring her.

Before she could stop him, he'd reached for her car door and had it open. He must've picked up the keys as well as the flowers.

"I'm not sure about your choice in a new car, honey. It's a little on the big side for you, isn't it?" There was soft admonishment in his tone. It sent a shiver of fear slicing down her spine.

Penny gaped at him. She hadn't seen Mitch in nearly two years, and all he could talk about was her choice of car. But then again, that was exactly Mitch's modus operandi. To belittle and criticize every single thing she did and said. She'd chosen this older model Hyundai Tucson because it was cheap, and was big enough to handle the dirt roads out on the ranch. But that was beside the point.

"Get away from me, and get away from my car," she ground out from between gritted teeth.

He took two, quick steps closer, pinning her against the rear door of the car.

"Now why would I want to do that, honey? You're my wife. I've come to bring you home. So, I don't want to hear any more of your demands to get away from you. You hear me?"

His hard, male body pushed against hers as he leaned his face in close. A pulse of adrenaline spiked through her belly and the old fear threatened to take hold once more. One of his hands snaked up around her throat. He wasn't choking her; it was more of a caress. But the threat was implied. The feel of his hands on her skin made her stomach roil.

"We're both going to get into this car of yours, and I'm going to drive you home to Santa Barbara, and we're going to forget this whole little interlude ever happened. What do you say?"

Penny shook her head. No. No, she couldn't do that. Wouldn't do that.

His grip on her throat tightened.

Mitch had only ever gotten physical with her once in their whole four years of marriage. And he'd been terribly apologetic afterward. He didn't believe in physical violence. His form of control was much more subtle and undermining.

"Mitch, leave me alone." It was hard to squeeze the words past his hand at her throat. She was aghast at how raspy and thin her voice sounded. He would never do as she asked. Not when she sounded so insipid.

Once before, she'd been able to find her voice. Find her courage and screw it up so tight that she was able to leave him. Sneak away in the dead of night. That courage seemed to abandon her now, however. She drew in another gasp, but the words wouldn't come.

"I think you should do as the lady says," a deep voice said from Penny's left, toward the rear of the car. It took both of them by surprise, and Mitch loosened his grip as he turned to stare at whoever had spoken. Penny was quick to recover her wits, using Mitch's distraction to slip out from between him and the car, moving rapidly away.

It was Clayton.

Neither of them had heard him approach. He was standing a few feet away, hands held loosely by his sides, a furrow appearing on his forehead as he glared at Mitch.

Penny sucked in a fortifying breath. And then another. Mitch spun around, as if to come toward her again, and she moved nearer to Clayton. Not hiding behind him exactly, but using his presence as a shield.

"Sorry, dude, but this is none of your business." Mitch gave one of his charming, boyish smiles. "I'm just having a little conversation with my wife here."

Clayton shot her a quick glance, one eyebrow lifted. But then went back to staring at Mitch. His easy stance never changed; his white Stetson was tipped in a relaxed style, his jeans and white T making him look completely approachable, like he was out having a friendly chat with a neighbor. But there was an aura of restrained violence surrounding him. That aura of violence wasn't just for show. Clayton had spent time in prison. He knew how to protect himself. Mitch had better be careful.

"Whatever you're doing, and whoever you are, this lady doesn't want to talk to you. So, you'd best do as she asks." Clayton's voice wasn't angry or aggressive. Penny had heard him use that tone on a recalcitrant heifer back when he worked on the ranch. Encouraging, but firm. He would not take *no* for an answer.

Mitch glanced at Penny and then back at Clayton. The anger had left his face, his eyes now hooded, the monster once again hidden. Mitch always was a coward. He only bullied those weaker than him. If an alpha male confronted him—like Clayton was doing right now—he'd always back away.

Penny crossed her arms and fortified herself with a few quick breaths. She needed to make sure her ex-husband got the message once and for all.

"You'd better leave town, Mitch. Now. I'm going straight to the cops. If you break the restraining order again, they'll lock you up." She knew it'd take a lot more than one little break of a restraining order to have him locked up—one police officer had all but admitted openly that even with that piece of paper, they couldn't do more than slap him on the wrist if he were caught breaking it—but she hoped her bluff might work.

Mitch raised his hands placatingly in the air and his shoulders fell. He looked her straight in the eye. "Is it true, Penny? Do you really want nothing more to do with me?"

"It's completely true. I want you gone from my life, Mitch," she said. She could see Clayton out of the corner of her eye, watching and waiting but not interfering. Like her own personal guardian angel.

"Consider it done then. I'll go home and sign the divorce papers tomorrow."

What? Would he really do that? Or was it too good to be true?

"Good," she replied firmly.

Mitch stared at her, looking more like a puppy she'd kicked than the manipulative bastard she knew him to be. But she'd never be fooled by his façade again. He turned, and without another word, walked toward the corner of the parking lot. She could make out the front bumper of a vehicle poking its nose out of a side alley. She and Clayton watched in silence as Mitch got into the car and drove slowly away. He'd obviously parked in the alley and lain in wait for her to come out of the florist. But how had he known where she'd be?

"You okay?" Clayton's deep voice was gravelly and full of concern. She felt all the adrenaline depart her body in an almighty rush, leaving her shaking and feeling faint.

"I don't know," she said, hearing the wobble in her voice and hating it.

To his credit, Clayton didn't ask all the questions she knew must be burning in his mind. Instead, he said, "My truck is over there. Do you want to come and sit for a while? You look pale. I don't think you should drive right now." Clayton pointed to his old, blue truck, pulled up on the verge at the back of the parking lot. "I was driving by and I saw you. I didn't like the look of that guy. So, I stopped." He came and stood close to her shoulder, but didn't try to touch her. For which she was eternally grateful. Her entire body was in overdrive; ultra-sensitive, so full of unresolved tension that if he touched her, she might well have screamed.

After a moment's hesitation, she said, "Yes, please. That would be good." He was right, there was no way she should drive in her current state. If she took a few moments to compose herself, maybe she'd be all right to go back to the ranch.

"Wait here," he commanded, then he jogged toward his truck.

She leaned against her car for support, gaze anxiously flicking left and right. What if Mitch came back? What if his words had all been a pretense, and he wasn't going home like he said? But no, he wouldn't approach her now, not with Clayton still around. Her mind was whirling a million miles an hour, unable to settle on even one coherent thought.

Clayton's pickup pulled up next to her and he ran around and opened the door for her, beckoning her inside. She needed to sit down before she fell. Confirming that the flowers were safely locked inside her car, she lurched toward the offered comfort of the truck cab, but her feet weren't completely under her own control. Clayton watched her warily, as if ready to scoop her up in his arms if she started to fall. But that would never do. So, Penny steeled herself and put one foot in front of the other until Clayton had her by the hand and was helping her up onto the bench seat. She sank into the old leather gratefully, leaning forward and covering her face with her hands.

Sudden tears pricked at the back of her eyelids. She willed them away. Now wasn't the time to burst into tears. Later, she would allow herself that luxury. Right now, she had to stay calm and logical. She pushed the heels of her palms harder into her eye sockets. Clayton got into the driver's side, but said nothing for a few seconds, until she felt his warm palm against the bare skin of her arm. There was compassion in that touch.

"You look like you could do with a drink and someone to talk to," he said.

She couldn't go back to the ranch in this state.

Actually, she might never go back. Now that Mitch knew where she was, she needed to get away from here. Move on. Find another place to hide.

"My house is only a few blocks from here. I've got whiskey and beer," Clayton continued. "As long as you don't mind…" He hesitated. "Well, you know about my reputation. As long as you're not bothered by being in my truck. By being seen with me."

Penny lowered her hands and turned to stare at him. Clayton's blue eyes fixed on hers, never wavering. The idea that she shouldn't be getting into Clayton's truck had never crossed her mind. Clayton had only ever been kind to her. Back when he'd worked as a cowboy on the ranch, before all the horrible business with the arsonist fires, he'd flirted with her. And she'd flirted back. She'd never have gone out with him, of course, because back then, her life had been a complete mess.

She'd only escaped from Mitch a few months beforehand, and there was no way she would even consider dating. It was too risky. When Naomi had offered her the job as a receptionist at Stargazer, it'd been a godsend. Somewhere to hide out and lick her wounds, get over Mitch. She'd never planned on staying so long, but days had turned into weeks, then into months and years.

Clayton had been the quintessential Montana cowboy. Larger than life, so sure of himself. And gorgeous. With his ice-blue eyes, thick head of nut-brown hair and bulging biceps that begged to be wrapped around her, what was there not to like?

But Clayton had been accused of lighting the fires plaguing Stargazer Ranch. And instead of facing the charges head on, he'd disappeared. Went on the run. Which had made him look even more guilty.

To make matters worse, he'd tried to kidnap Cat in a rash attempt to clear his name.

Clayton had been found not guilty of arson when they finally charged Alex Donovan, another ranch employee in regards to the fires. But people had remained suspicious of Clayton and so, less than a month after Alex's arrest, when more arson fires were lit, they'd again looked upon him with unfriendly eyes. It turned out Alex's brother Cyrus, had taken it upon himself to try and finish the job Alex had started, and he was eventually caught and incarcerated, as well. But Clayton had still spent another six months—taking into account his time already served—in jail for his attempted abduction charges. Now he'd returned to Stevensville, supposedly to put his life back on track.

Penny stared at him, pursing her lips. Could he really be trusted?

CHAPTER TWO

Clayton couldn't believe he'd suggested Penny come back to his place. What a dumb thing to do. But she seemed so upset and confused. All he wanted was to comfort her. He waited for her to refuse his offer. To say thanks, but no thanks. It was what she should do. It was what every self-respecting local in Stevensville had already done. Clayton saw the looks they cast as he walked by them on the pathway. The way they whispered behind their hands. Or not; some were brazen enough to stare at him in public, letting their disapproval and disgust show for all to see. He wasn't wanted here in town. People didn't trust him.

She bit her bottom lip as she studied him and goddamn, he knew he shouldn't let it, but she was turning him on. She had this kind of teachers' vibe, with her long, blonde hair always pulled back in a decorous braid, as well as those thick, black glasses she wore. But she wasn't fooling him. He could see those wickedly sexy curves she tried to camouflage beneath her jeans and loose-fitting tops.

Finally, letting go of her lip, she said, "I don't think it's a good idea for me to go back to the ranch until I calm down. And I could do with a whiskey." She hesitated. "Besides, we're friends, aren't we?" When he nodded in reply, she continued, "So, I don't have a problem, if you don't."

"Yes, ma'am." He started his truck and pulled slowly out of the parking lot.

Clayton knew little about Penny. One thing he did know was that she'd been one of the few people who hadn't shied away from him when he first returned after his stint in jail. Whenever she went past him in town, she'd make a point to stop and talk to him. She'd even been instrumental in helping him find a job. It wasn't the best job in the world, hauling lumber and stocking the warehouse for Butterby's renovation and building company over near the highway. Penny had heard about the job when the company manager mentioned to Dean, the owner of Stargazer, that he was looking to hire, if he knew anyone who was interested. Penny had piped up and offered the manger Clayton's name, much to Dean's surprise. He'd found all this out later through George, the foreman. It wasn't what he dreamed he'd be doing at this stage of his life. But for a convicted felon fresh out of prison, he was damn lucky to have it.

It was nice to know someone was willing to stand up for him. To vouch for his good character when most people still thought his name was mud.

Perhaps they were right. Perhaps he deserved their condemnation. His thoughts were so mixed up these days, even he didn't know if he was a good guy or not, anymore.

Clayton glanced over at Penny in the passenger seat. Her hands were tightly clasped together, and she stared out the windshield as if not seeing the passing scenery. He drove with the widows down, letting in a cool blast of air. The heat of the Montana summer day was fading now that the sun was diving toward the horizon and the Bitterroot Mountains, but the air still held a balmy tinge. His eyes were drawn to the way her simple black top showed off her bare shoulders.

Who was that guy in the parking lot? He was pretty sure

Penny had never mentioned a husband, or even an ex-husband, back when he'd been working on the ranch. What was she hiding?

The drive to his house only took a few minutes, but when he pulled up in the driveway, Penny remained motionless, still staring through the windshield. He went around and opened her door.

"We're here," he said gently. Penny started, as if she'd been lost somewhere else entirely and had only just realized he was standing next to her. She followed him silently along the drive and then up the front steps to his battered, old porch.

Clayton glanced around the front yard as he sorted through his keys. It was full of weeds and disuse. He really should do something about that. The Montana Department of Corrections had a reentry program that lent a hand to all newly released felons. They'd helped find him this house with cheap rent and also paired him up with another recently released inmate to share the load. He hoped Harry wasn't home. He usually took his two daughters out for a meal on Tuesday nights.

Clayton opened the door and switched on a light, leading Penny straight to the kitchen. He dropped his Stetson on a side countertop. Harry had left it in a mess, which wasn't unusual, and Clayton wanted to curse the man. But Penny didn't seem to notice; she sank into the nearest chair at the small kitchen table. Her normally vibrant face was clouded, her eyes glazed over. Penny had the most amazing eyes; they were enough to floor a man on the spot. Clayton had often thought they reminded him of the ocean, sometimes a blue-green, when she was happy, which often faded to a gray if her mood was low. Like right now. Her eyes were hooded tonight, the color of a storm-tossed sea. She looked like she was in shock, and Clayton wondered again who that guy in the parking lot was and why he'd affected her this way.

Penny's car had attracted his attention as he was driving by. Then he'd seen her, backed up against the rear of her car, with a man standing over her. His guts had twisted at the sight, and he knew something was wrong. So, he'd swung his truck around on the road and parked it up on the edge. He hadn't been sure if Penny would welcome his interference, but he was prepared to face her wrath if he'd gotten it wrong.

The bottle of whiskey was kept hidden from Harry, tucked in behind the cleaning products the other man never used underneath the sink—Harry was supposed to be attending AA, but he still refused to believe he had a problem. Clayton pulled it out and put two glasses on the table in front of Penny.

"Here you go," he said, handing her one. "I hope you like it neat, I haven't got anything to mix it with."

Penny lifted her chin to stare up at the glass, as if seeing him for the first time. "Thank you," was all she said, before downing the shot with one quick flick of her wrist.

Wow, she must've really needed that drink. Clayton threw his drink back as well and enjoyed the quick burn as it hit the back of his throat.

"Another," she demanded, banging the glass on the wooden tabletop. "Please," she added belatedly when he hesitated.

"Okay." He poured them both another one and took the seat opposite, watching as she swallowed this in a single gulp as well.

He drank his second a lot slower as he continued to watch her.

"Thank you. I needed that," she said, rubbing a hand across her face, pushing her long bangs irritably out of her eyes. "Can I have another, please?"

"Are you sure?" Worry tugged at the fringes of Clayton's mind. The last thing he needed was a woman passed out in his living room. Even though he required no parole after his release, he knew the cops might not look kindly on that kind of thing.

"Yes." She nodded, and he refilled her glass. This time, she sipped at it, and he let out a quiet breath. "I need to thank you for stopping. For rescuing me." The last part was said awkwardly, as if Penny were loath to admit she'd needed help.

"Coming to the rescue of a damsel in distress isn't usually my style." He gave a self-effacing grin. "But for you, I made an exception." He tried to make light of the matter; to shy away from the heart of the conversation. Because most people would probably think it more than a little ironic that he had come to Penny's rescue after what he did to Cat. After he tried to abduct her. His insides curdled into knots of self-condemnation. How could he have considered such a thing? Even as desperate as he was, Clayton now knew it'd been the single most stupid, irresponsible, and barbaric thing he'd ever done. It'd been the lowest point of his life.

"Well, you did a good thing. I'm not sure what would've happened if you hadn't come along." Penny's pretty face crumpled, and it looked like she might cry. But she rubbed the back of her hand across her eyes and sat up straighter.

"Do you mind if I ask who that guy was?" When she didn't answer, he added, "You know, in case I need to send him packing again."

She looked at him with her stormy eyes, considering. Finally, she flicked her long braid over her shoulder, and said, "Hardly anyone knows, but I guess the cat's out of the bag now. If you pour me one more drink, I'll tell you."

He hesitated, and she said, "I promise, this will be my last. I need it, if you're going to hear all the sordid details of my past."

He poured her another but left his own glass empty. One of

them needed to stay sober.

"That man is my ex-husband. Well, technically he's still my husband, because he won't sign the divorce papers. But in my mind, I haven't been married to him for the past two years."

Clayton was a little confused. "Why won't he divorce you? If that's what you want? He can't still be hoping you'll go back to him?"

"Sadly, that's exactly what he thinks. Mitch is… I'm not really sure how to explain Mitch. He's a complicated man." Penny took a small sip of whiskey and leaned her elbows on the table. There was a slight slurring to her voice, the only indication that the alcohol was having an effect.

"We got married when I was twenty-five. I thought I was old enough then to know what I was doing. What I was getting myself into." She shook her head. "Nothing could've been farther from the truth. But it took me four years of trying to make things work with him, to finally realize what a manipulative bastard he really is." She took another slow sip, her face ashen as she seemingly relived those four years.

Her comment had him wondering how old she was. She could pass for mid-twenties, easily. But from what she'd just said, she must be at least thirty. Which put her much closer to his own age. He'd flirted with her back at the ranch because he'd thought she was pretty and smart, and because it did his ego good to see her come out of her shell and flirt back. But he'd always thought she was too young—and a class above him—to ever take him seriously.

"What do you mean?" He prompted, suddenly hit by an icy fear. "He didn't hurt you? Strike you?"

"No," she said a little too sharply. "Mitch wasn't physically violent toward me."

"So, why did you…?"

"You mean, why did I marry him in the first place?"

Clayton nodded.

"Mitch came across as such a kind and compassionate person, at first. He always showered me with gifts. Roses, chocolate, nights out. He even took me on a surprise holiday to Hawaii, after we'd only been dating for three months."

"So, he swept you off your feet?" Clayton prompted.

She took another sip before answering him. "Yes. And no. I was aware he had certain problems. He never made a secret of the abuse he suffered as a child. His mother used to hit him and make him feel useless. He once told me she made him feel smaller than a piece of dirt buried in the heel of her shoe."

"He was appealing to your better nature, then. Making you feel sympathetic, so you'd like him." Clayton clenched his fists on the tabletop. This guy sounded like a slimy worm. Personally, he would never use his own misfortune to try to sway a woman his way. If anything, he was the complete opposite.

"Exactly. He used the story of his terrible childhood to suck me in further. And it worked. I felt so sorry for him. And I appreciated that he'd risen above all that, was trying to become a better man."

Clayton was absorbed by her story. He could imagine that man back in the parking lot, working his magic on a young and naïve Penny. She had a kind soul. Was sensitive and warm. Perhaps a little too on the altruistic side. And her ex was handsome, which made it easier to get women to believe him. No one liked to think a handsome man was capable of anything underhanded.

"It sounds like that was all a cover-up. He wasn't a better man at all?"

Penny shook her head.

"No. It started out subtly enough, Mitch used to complain that I talked to my sister on the phone too much."

Clayton lifted an eyebrow. While it was true some women

talked incessantly on the phone—his own two sisters were an excellent case in point—it didn't seem like something any man could get in the way of. And he wouldn't try. Even if his sisters often talked endlessly about him, and tried to solve his problems for him, they saw it as helping. He saw it as interfering, but he'd never dream of telling them to stop.

Penny continued, "Then came the chronic criticism. Small things at first, like how I didn't hold my fork properly. Or he didn't like the new throw rug and cushions I'd bought for the living room." Penny wrinkled her cute nose, and his gaze was momentarily trapped by the way she rolled her mouth into a soft pout.

"Mitch became paranoid and suspicious of everyone I talked to. I couldn't even wave at the postman without attracting his comments. It felt like I was walking on eggshells all the time." Her glass was empty, and she rolled it between her fingers as she spoke. "He'd say things like, *"If you'd actually finished college, you might have something to talk about with my friends, and then you wouldn't feel so left out."* or if I was late getting home one night, *"If you can't even be bothered to make dinner, I don't even know what I'm getting from this relationship."*

"He sounds like a real charmer," Clayton growled softly. It never ceased to amaze him that strong, feisty women like Penny would ever put up with that kind of thing. He knew other women, who let their self-esteem become ground down each and every day by an unappreciative husband. Clayton swore that if he was ever lucky enough to get married—which seemed highly unlikely now—that he would treat his wife with respect and decency. Like an equal, not a servant.

"Yeah," Penny replied sardonically. "Then came the threats that if I ever left him, I'd never see a dollar from the house we bought together. He said he'd lock up our accounts so tight, I'd never have access to any money. That I'd end up alone.

That nobody would want a loser like me."

Clayton wanted to say, how dare he do that. But sadly, he knew it happened all over the country. It was one tactic men used to make themselves feel powerful. Until now, he'd always been outraged when he heard this kind of thing, but it'd never touched him personally. Seeing how cruelly it affected Penny threw it all into a new light for him.

"His last threats were the worst. But they weren't threats to me, they were threats to himself. That he'd harm himself if I ever left. That he could never live without me."

"He really said that?" Clayton got up and stalked over to the sink. This guy sounded like a complete dick, and he couldn't sit still any longer listening to Penny talk about him.

"Yes," Penny said in a small voice.

"And you believed he'd do it?" he rumbled menacingly. He wanted to go and smack some sense into the man. No one should have that kind of burden thrust on them by someone else; have it hanging over their head. What an absolute loser.

"For a long time, I did, yes." Penny was staring out the small kitchen window, that glazed look returning into her face. "Until I decided that he was being unfair, that his life shouldn't be in my hands, and I finally found the strength to run away. Start a new life. But now he's found me, I'm worried I'll have to move again. He's going to try to force me to go home with him. I can't do that, I just can't." She sounded so lost and alone, her face was so wretched, that he wanted to hug her. A strange heat curled up from deep within his belly, and he wanted to punch that guy in the face. Wanted to protect Penny. To wrap her in his arms and not let any anguish touch her. He wanted to tell her she didn't have to do this alone.

But what could he do to help? Nothing. Because he was a convicted felon, and if he so much as touched a hair on that guy's head, he'd be headed straight back to jail.

CHAPTER THREE

Clayton was looking at her with pity in his eyes. She hated to be pitied. How could she ever explain the hold Mitch had had over her? Still had over her. The guilt that ate away at her insides at the thought he might, indeed, hurt himself. No one fully understood. Bethany, her younger sister, had helped her to leave Mitch, but not even she knew the full extent of his lies and deceits. Of how Penny was completely terrified of what he'd do next. And she also had no idea of Penny's whereabouts. They both knew it was safer that way; then Mitch couldn't extort the information from her.

And that was why she had to do this alone. No one else was going to help her out of this hole she'd dug herself in to.

Penny glanced up at the kitchen clock hanging above the sink.

"Holy cow, I need to get back to the ranch." She stood up quickly as she realized the time and then clapped a hand to her head when it began to spin. Too much whiskey.

Clayton put out a hand to steady her. His fingers were warm and certain on her arm.

"I'm fine," she replied after taking hold of the edge of the table. "Can you take me back to my car, please?"

"You're in no state to drive," he said, letting her arm go

slowly, once he was sure she was stable. He leaned back against the countertop and crossed his arms, that small furrow back between his eyes as he contemplated her.

Oh, God. Look how big his biceps were when he crossed his arms that way. Penny couldn't tear her gaze away. They were amazing, bulging out of the sleeves of his T-shirt in a way that had her hanging on to the table with her other hand, before she was knocked over by the sight.

She'd completely forgotten what they'd been talking about.

"Did you hear me? I'm not going to let you drive in your condition."

Oh, right, they'd been discussing her getting home. Her mind was fuzzy, the whiskey making her thoughts skitter like a cat on marbles. All she could see clearly was those biceps curled in tight to a very impressive chest. Mmm, how would it feel to run her fingers lightly across—

"I'll take you back to the ranch."

"What?" Her eyes sprang back to his, hoping she hadn't been caught staring. Drooling, really.

"I'll drive you out. You can make arrangements to collect your car later."

That's right, her car was still in the parking lot.

"Oh my, the flowers." She put a hand up to her mouth. She'd completely forgotten about the flowers, too. It seemed Clayton and drinking were two things she needed to avoid from now on if she wanted to keep her wits about her. She needed to get the flowers back to the ranch. At least they were safe in the back of her car.

When Mitch had first appeared beside her car, Penny's first instinct had been to run. And it still was. She should get out of Stevensville as soon as possible. But like Clayton said, she was in no state to drive and no state to make big decisions, either. She'd go back to the ranch, at least for tonight, and think about what her next steps should be. She needed to accept Clayton's help tonight, too, whether she liked it or not.

"We'll pick up your flowers on the way."

"Thank you." She hung her head and dropped her shoulders. She didn't want to seem ungrateful. All Clayton had ever done was offer her help.

They drove in silence back to the florist, and Clayton helped her transfer the bunches of flowers into his truck.

"They're samples for Cat and Levi's wedding," she said by way of explanation, then cursed inwardly as he flinched at the mention of Cat. Blaming the whiskey for loosening her tongue, she decided she couldn't help it if she was Cat's friend, and a bridesmaid in her wedding. Clayton would have to deal with it.

"I heard they're getting married at the ranch," he said, sliding into the truck beside her.

"Yes, in a few days' time," she replied, carefully laying the flowers between them on the bench seat next to his Stetson, surreptitiously studying him from beneath her lashes.

"That's good. They suit each other. They make a great couple."

There was no spite or bitterness in his tone. It almost sounded as if he were happy for them. As if he regretted what he'd done. This revelation might surprise others, but Penny had known all along that Clayton hadn't intended to hurt Cat. Which was why she trusted him when others didn't.

He drove out of the parking lot and she lay her head against the backrest. It was good Clayton hadn't let her drive, the world was still spinning slightly, and she wasn't in full control of her faculties.

She snatched a quick glance at Clayton, his big hands on the wheel, chestnut hair slicked back by the breeze from the open window, one elbow leaning on the sill as he drove. She couldn't decide if she liked him better with his hat on or off. That hat certainly gave him a maverick vibe. Back when

Clayton had worked at Stargazer, he'd always seemed so… dauntless. He was quick with a wink and that sexy, crooked smile which had her melting at the knees. Nothing had seemed to scare Clayton. Stubborn and determined, he was like an unbroken bronco who could never be tamed.

Now, Clayton seemed shrunken, his fire and passion diminished. Which Penny found terribly sad. Life and circumstances had beaten him down.

But she could see echoes of herself in Clayton. Mitch had done a superb job at eroding her self-confidence until she'd questioned every single thing she thought or did. After she left him, she changed her appearance, hoping to throw him off the scent. Dyed her hair blonde and purchased non-prescription glasses. She'd had no problem with her eyesight but hoped the more severe, librarian, look would help her blend in. She'd also been terrified to trust anyone.

But her time at the ranch had seen her slowly learn to have faith again. To make friends. To believe she could have a future.

Bethany, was always asking if she was going to come home soon. Penny had been considering it. But with Mitch showing up, she knew it was too risky to go home.

It made her wonder about Clayton. He wasn't originally from Montana. Penny remembered him telling her he was born in Austin, Texas.

The words tumbled out of her mouth before she could filter them. "Why did you come back here? After you got out of prison? Why didn't you go home?" Holy cow, that came out a little blunter than she'd hoped. She gave him a bright smile when he cast her a bemused look. "Sorry, it's the whiskey talking," she said, waving a hand in the air.

"You're not the first person to ask me that," he replied, voice gruff. "And I'm not sure I can answer it." He lifted one shoulder in a shrug. The movement drew Penny's gaze to those broad shoulders, his back straight and firm in the driver's seat.

"There are lots of reasons I stayed here. The main one being that housing is cheap, and there are plenty of menial jobs for an ex-con." Penny shot him another glance. There must be more to it than that, but she merely gave him a sympathetic smile.

He tapped a finger on the steering wheel, as if trying to decide whether to go on. "I wasn't welcome at home. My father... Well, let's just say he thinks I've dragged the Sabitino family name through the mud, and he's not happy about it."

"Oh, I see." Penny felt a twist in her guts on Clayton's behalf. It must hurt to have your own father say that to you. Families could be complicated things at best, and at worst...

"And while my mom is more forgiving, she can't talk to me when my dad, is around."

Again, her heart went out to the man sitting across from her in the truck.

"It's probably better this way, if I stay away from them, and they stay away from me." Clayton didn't elaborate further, but she wondered at his relationship with his mother. Were they close? How could a mother forsake her son? But then, her own mother had chosen to turn a blind eye to what was happening between her and Mitch. It's not that she wasn't sympathetic when Penny first tentatively broached the subject about Mitch's abnormal control over her. It was more that she'd subtly implied perhaps Penny could try a little harder to make her marriage work. Her mother believed marriage was for life, not to be tossed away on frivolous flights of fancy or slight irritation. Penny had stopped complaining to her mother after the first few times, knowing she didn't want to understand.

Bethany had been her sounding board; she'd been the one who'd eventually talked Penny into making a plan to leave

Mitch. But even Bethany hadn't known the true depths Mitch had gone to maintain mastery over her. What he was genuinely capable of. Her sister was more than willing to help her escape, it was her own reluctance to put Bethany in any kind of danger that'd stopped her from getting any more involved.

At the thought of Bethany, Penny said, "Do you have any brothers or sisters?"

"You bet. I've got two sisters. Stacey is the youngest, she still lives in Austin and she offered me her couch if I ever needed it." Clayton's face softened at the mention of Stacey. "But she's married to a musician, they both like the alternative lifestyle and I'm not sure their house is big enough for me to live there with them like a hippy." He laughed, and she watched his mouth lift in the crooked smile she was coming to adore.

"What about the other sister?"

"Courtney lives in Houston with her rich, doctor husband and two kids. Although she's never said it out loud, I know I'm not the sort of undesirable she wants near her kids."

"Oh, okay." Penny was unsure how to go on. Perhaps it was better to just drop the subject altogether. Silence descended between them.

Clayton drove the country road with his high beams on, for good reason. There were plenty of wild critters that came out after dark, especially on the warm, Montana summer nights. Penny had seen her share of bats and owls, and even large moths that became active on the ranch after the sun went down. Jackrabbits and foxes were a common sight on these country roads at night. But it was the larger animals like the deer, or perhaps even a bear, which could be deadly if you hit them. Penny had come close a few times, which was one reason she tried to stay off the roads at night, if she could help it.

The headlights cut a blade of light through the dark night. Clayton slowed the pickup as they crested a hill, and the large, stone wall marking the entrance to Stargazer Ranch appeared. He guided the truck smoothly onto the dirt, and Penny drew in a deep breath of clean, mountain air.

Dean had built twenty luxury cabins on the property, all completely secluded, just the way the guests liked it, and soon the individual log cabins were slipping past on either side. People came all year round to enjoy the many activities and holiday lifestyle the resort offered, like horseback riding or hiking in the summer, or skiing and dog sledding in the winter. The truck threaded through a tunnel of overhanging branches and emerged into a darkened, open area of rolling hills and fields. And there, nestled in a valley, sat the main lodge, its lights twinkling like a fairy doll house. With its soaring ceilings and many large windows to take in the views, it was so beautiful it nearly took Penny's breath away every time she saw it.

To Penny, the ranch was a haven. A place where she'd felt safe; at least, until tonight. It felt like she was coming home.

"Do you miss working here?" The words were out of her mouth before she could think them through, and she clapped a hand over her face. Holy cow, what must he think of her? She shouldn't drink whiskey; it did odd things to her inhibitions. "Oh, I'm sorry, forget I asked that," she said apologetically.

Clayton's gaze remained fixed on the road, but his lips thinned, and that furrow was back between his eyes, deeper this time. Crap, she'd really upset him.

"Yeah, I do miss working here." His admission took her completely by surprise. "This was my dream job," he continued. "I loved the ranch life, the horses. I was even aiming to buy my own dude ranch one day. But I guess we all have dreams that weren't meant to be, right?"

"I guess so." It was true, most of her dreams had been shattered when she left Mitch, her marriage, and her house behind.

How sad for Clayton, though. That he'd been forced to give up the one true job he loved. It didn't seem fair that just because Alex had framed him for the fires, Clayton was still suffering. But Penny conceded that he hadn't exactly acted in an exemplary manner. Running away from the cops after Levi's house was set on fire made it look as if he were guilty. And then trying to solve his problems by force. He'd certainly mucked that one up when he'd tried to abduct Cat, even if it had only been a misguided attempt to clear his name.

They were nearly at the lodge.

"Are you going to go to the cops? Report your ex?" Clayton asked, as he pulled to a smooth stop in front of the stone steps leading up to the main lodge.

Penny hadn't considered that question yet. There were lots of things she needed to decide. Top priority was whether to stay or go.

"Probably not," she finally admitted. "It won't make any difference. The cops practically said as much back when I first had the restraining order issued."

"But at least it will go on file that he's been harassing you. It's better to let them know, maybe they can keep an eye on him."

"Maybe." She sat with her hand on the door handle, ready to exit the truck. "I'll think about it," she promised. And she would, but she couldn't guarantee she'd still be here tomorrow to make that report to the police. She opened the door and prepared to gather her flowers and handbag.

"Would you mind keeping this all to yourself, please?" Penny looked at Clayton properly for the first time since they'd got into his truck. "Nobody at the ranch knows. About Mitch, I mean."

He studied her, blue eyes reflecting the overhead cabin light. "If that's what you want," he finally answered.

"Thank you," she said, hopping down from the truck, arms full of flowers. "You saved me today. I'm not sure what…" She couldn't finish her sentence, because what would've happened if Clayton hadn't come along? Would she be sitting in her car, as Mitch drove her home to Santa Barbara, even now? A shiver ran through her body at that thought.

"No problem," came his simple reply. "If you ever need me again, don't hesitate. Okay?" He fixed her with her steady gaze. "I mean it. You've got my cell number."

She nodded mutely, a lump suddenly forming in her throat at the thought that he cared enough to want to help. They'd exchanged numbers back at his house, Clayton had said as a precaution if Mitch ever came near her again.

She closed the door and watched him drive away. Confusion still surrounded her feelings for Clayton. Didn't everyone deserve the benefit of the doubt? But look where that'd gotten her with Mitch. She'd given him a second chance, and then a third and fourth, until it was never ending. She was damned if she was going to make the same mistake ever again.

From now on, it was probably better if she stayed as far away from Clayton as possible. He was just one more complication she didn't need in her life right now.

CHAPTER FOUR

Clayton drove slowly down the gravel driveway, watching Penny's dark silhouette in his rear vision mirror as she walked up the steps. At least she was calmer, seemed to have regained her self-control. That bastard had really rattled her. Why were some men such dickheads? Would the ex do as he said, and go home and sign the divorce papers and leave Penny alone? He'd seemed pretty convincing to Clayton, but Penny didn't appear so sure.

He wondered what she would do next. He hoped she decided to stay. He liked her. Not that that would have any sway over the matter. The look in her eyes made him believe she'd probably run. And he couldn't blame her. After all, he'd been the first one to run away at the earliest sign of trouble. Never again. He was resolved to stand and face his problems from now on. Back then, he'd been a different man. Bold and full of himself. So brash he believed he could outfox the cops, clear his own name without any help. Fat lot of good that'd done him.

He shouldn't get involved with her. There were enough troubles on his own plate to deal with, he didn't need to be sucked into hers, too.

Troubles like the two men he'd seen hanging around the

back dock of the delivery yard, yesterday. Clayton had alerted the foreman when he noticed them. George didn't take kindly to anyone lurking around the yard. When George had gone to ask them if they needed help, they'd fobbed him off with some story about sizing up lumber for a backyard fence they were thinking of building. George had asked them to meet him around at the front office, where he could draw them up a quote. But when he got there, the men had disappeared. Jumped in their black sedan and driven off.

The incident had left Clayton with all kinds of caution signs flashing in his head. The men had been dressed in plaid and jeans, to make it look like they belonged with the rest of the local clientele. But there was something off about them. Perhaps their hair was too well-groomed. Or their eyes were too sharp. Whatever it was, Clayton didn't believe they were simply looking for timber, not for one second. Which meant they could possibly be Dmytro's boys, sniffing around.

Clayton had drawn back behind a large, concrete pillar when he first saw them, hoping they hadn't spotted him. Then he'd melted into the dark loading dock, gone straight to tell George. Should he follow the advice he'd given to Penny, and have a chat with Deputy Wilder, down at the sheriff's office? But what would he say? He had no concrete evidence. Just a gut instinct, and that usually bought you exactly zero when it came to getting a cop to do something.

His distrust of cops ran deep. After what they'd done to him, how they'd tried to pin those terrible arson attacks on him, who could blame him? Jude Wilder was the best of a bad bunch, but at least he listened to Clayton. He was close in age to Clayton and they'd been sort of buddies before the fires eighteen months ago, frequented the same bars, mixed in a similar circle of friends.

Nah, it was getting late, and the sheriff's office was clear on the other side of town. He couldn't be bothered to drive over there. He was almost home now. Perhaps he'd report it tomorrow.

Harry must be back from dining with his kids. The lights were on in the house when Clayton pulled up in the driveway.

He banged in through the door and threw his keys on the hallway table, along with his Stetson. "Harry, you home?" he called.

"In the kitchen."

Clayton rounded through the doorway and stopped in his tracks. Shit, he'd forgotten to hide the whiskey before he took Penny home. Harry was sitting at the table, pouring himself a glass. And he looked pretty happy, which meant he'd already had quite a few. The only solution to stop his roommate from finishing the entire bottle was to drink it, as well.

He didn't ask if Harry minded; it was his whiskey, after all. Clayton merely sat and poured himself a big slug.

"Did you have a good night?" he asked conversationally.

"Me and the girls had a grand night. I took them to that new place up near the river crossing." Harry looked at him through his thick-rimmed glasses, owl-like. He was an everyday kind of man, balding somewhat on top, but in typical fashion, he kept his brown hair a little longer, so he could comb it over and across. Smaller in stature than Clayton, he liked to boast that he was nearly six foot, and Clayton bit his tongue every time he said it, because he clearly wasn't anywhere near Clayton's six-foot-two height. Harry also had this really, really annoying habit of winking. Perhaps he thought it made him more likable, but it had the opposite effect, making him look sleazy and eccentric.

And he employed that irritating mannerism right now. Winking, he said, "But before we get into what I did tonight, I've got a question for you."

"Fire away." Clayton downed half his glass. There was no

need to stay sober. Apart from having to get up in the morning, he had nowhere else to be.

"Why were there two glasses on the table?"

Clayton froze. Hell, he'd been sprung. Momentarily, he considered lying, but a quick glance at his glass told him there was a trace of pink lip gloss around the rim. Harry wasn't stupid, he wouldn't have missed that little jewel of a detail.

"I was helping out a friend. She had a run-in with her ex-husband, and she was a bit shook up. So, I brought her back here to let her calm down."

"You had a woman here? At the house?" Harry's sharp reply had Clayton looking up. "Do you think that's wise? After your conviction, and all?"

Harry was only speaking sense, but somehow it enraged Clayton. The same thought had crossed his mind, even as he helped Penny into his truck to bring her here. But he couldn't very well have left her out there, alone and in distress, wondering if her stupid dick of a husband was going to come back. What right did Harry have to tell him what to do?

Clayton poured himself another dose of whiskey, emptying the bottle. Harry pursed his lips as he watched the last drop go into Clayton's glass, but wisely said nothing.

"She's just a friend. If I can't help a friend, then there's something seriously wrong with the world."

"Hmm," Harry replied thoughtfully. "I'm not sure the cops would see it that way, but anyhow."

Why did the man have to be so smug all the time? Clayton had served his time and been let out a free man after over a year in prison. Some people said that a year wasn't long enough for his attempted abduction of Cat, that he was a danger to the community, and he should've been given much longer. Or at least been put on parole. Thankfully, the Department of Corrections didn't see it that way. They had, after all, wrongly charged him for arson, which triggered his ill-conceived abduction attempt in the first place.

Silence settled over the kitchen as Clayton nursed his last drink and his thoughts drifted back over the past few days.

He should probably warn Harry; they shared a house, after all. "You might want to watch your back over the next few days."

"What do you mean?" The small man narrowed his eyes at Clayton.

"I saw a couple of guys hanging around the warehouse today."

The man might look ordinary and unsophisticated, but he had a mind like a steel trap, and he picked up right away on Clayton's meaning. "You think they might be Dmytro's boys?"

"Maybe. Who knows?" Clayton shrugged and took another slug of whiskey.

Harry made a rude sound at the back of his throat. "I know I've already said this, but I'll never understand why you went to the cops. Have you got a martyr complex or something?" The other man slammed his empty glass down on the table. "Why would you put yourself out like that?"

Clayton shrugged again. He didn't expect the little lawyer to understand his motivations. Hell, *he* almost didn't understand his motives. But when he'd heard what Dmytro had done to Levi's brother, Wyatt, and that cute little French chef from the ranch, well, he'd seen red. Dymtro had sent thugs who tried to kill them to retrieve his stolen, black-market diamonds. Chased them all over the Bitterroot Mountains, terrorizing other innocent citizens in the process. All they'd done was to be in the wrong place at the wrong time.

Dmytro was a bastard who deserved to stay behind bars for the rest of his natural life. That was reason enough, surely? Dmytro's diamond disaster had been nearly six months ago. Clayton had fronted up to Jude and told him that if they needed more evidence to put Dmytro away for good, then he might be able to help. Jude had been only too happy to take a sworn affidavit from Clayton about his dealings on the inside with the mob boss. Clayton had asked Jude to keep his name out of it. Jude understood that Clayton could well be putting himself in danger by telling them what he knew, so he promised that Dmytro would never find out where the info had come from. But Dmytro wasn't stupid. The mobster's trial for the kidnap and torture of Cat and Levi was due in court in two months. There would be a separate trial later on for his involvement in the murder of Tony, who'd once been Dmytro's fence, selling his goods on the black market.

"You've met him." Clayton didn't have to say the mob boss's name; they both knew who he meant. "Wouldn't you do something if you had some dirt on him?"

"Nope." Harry glared at Clayton, his eyebrows bristling belligerently. "I'd keep my mouth shut."

Yeah, well, you're a slimy weasel, so that doesn't really surprise me. Clayton was careful not to say the words out loud. The man had been convicted of fraud and embezzlement, so to lie was imbedded in his DNA.

"I'll keep my eyes peeled, then. I sure hope you haven't attracted undue attention. I need to keep my nose clean, for both my daughters' sake."

Clayton felt a twinge of guilt for perhaps involving Harry in this business. But he'd be damned if he'd let a small-minded man like Harry dictate his moral compass. The guy could move out and find somewhere else to live, if that's the way he felt. If those men had been scouts for Dmytro—and it was a big *if*—then Clayton would be their target, not Harry.

"I'm going to bed," Harry announced, taking his glass over

to the sink and washing it out under the tap, leaving the rest of the dishes still piled on the countertop. Clayton bit his tongue and said nothing, just nodded as Harry walked past.

Clayton sat and stared morosely into the dregs of the amber liquid. There was one other reason Clayton had gone to give Jude intelligence on Dmytro. A tiny hope that perhaps it might be a way back into the good books of folks around here. Karma, and all that shit. If he did a good deed, then perhaps it might come back and help soften people's reactions.

Clayton had been telling the absolute truth when he declared to Penny that working at Stargazer had been the best job he'd ever had. Somewhere, in a guarded part of his heart, he still longed to be back there. But there was no way Dean would employ him again. Not after what he'd done to his precious Cat. It was a pipe dream, and nothing more.

CHAPTER FIVE

Penny apologized to Naomi a dozen times for running late, hoping that she couldn't smell the whiskey on her breath. She lied and said her car had refused to start and it'd been pure luck that Clayton had driven by at the exact right time. Naomi was more concerned that Penny had been stranded alone by the side of the road and waved away her apologies. She was a lovely woman, and a great boss, and it caused a knot of pain in the middle of her chest that Penny was lying to her. Naomi promised she'd send Dale and Big Tom into town to pick up her car tomorrow.

Then they took the bunches of flowers down to the undercover area, beneath the large verandah, to see how they'd look tied to the huge poles that supported the three-story lodge. The reception was going to be held here, once the ceremony was over. Cat had asked if they could use one of the gorgeous, little clearings in Naomi's wilderness garden surrounding the lodge for the service. It would be perfect, with a few lines of white-shrouded chairs set up beneath the shade of the towering, fir trees. But they'd have to wait until morning before they could properly see if the flowers suited the glade Cat had in mind.

"The flowers are perfect," Naomi declared finally. The

bunches were made up mainly of Montana native blooms, mixed with a few simple white roses. There were the palest blue cornflowers, and clusters of white field daisies and things Penny didn't know the name of, combined with sprays of summer greenery. Cat's wedding bouquet would be a smaller version of these large bunches.

Once they'd made sure the bunches were in water so they didn't spoil, Penny was finally free to escape to the staff quarters. Whisky did not agree with her. Her head was pounding, and she took a couple of Advil and lay on her bed, staring at the ceiling, her mind whirling in circles. And that was where Stella found her an hour later, once dinner service had ended.

"Hi, Penny. Is everything okay? I heard your car broke down." Stella waltzed into the room, a big smile on her face. And why wouldn't she be smiling? Right after the wedding, Stella was moving into one of the new cabins Dean had commissioned for the staff, for married couples. Or engaged couples, as was the case with Stella and Wyatt. Builders were putting the finishing touches to them, and they'd be ready by the end of the month. Penny was sad to be losing her roommate; they'd become the best of friends. But Stella had been conspicuously missing over the last few months, spending most of her nights at Wyatt's house. Moving in together on the ranch would be good for both of them. Penny would likely be leaving the ranch, anyway. Her heart lurched in her chest at the thought.

While Penny was still contemplating life on the run again, the other girl said with a wicked gleam in her eye, "I also heard Clayton brought you home. Is that true?"

Penny shuffled back and leaned her shoulders against the wall behind her bed, using the movement to cover her sudden discomfort at the mention of Clayton. At the way he'd looked at her as she got out of the truck, like he could see through to her fears and inadequacies. But it didn't seem to bother him. Because he had his own shortcomings. He'd made bad decisions in his life, just as she had. They were two defective people, alike in so many ways. Those blue eyes examining her had left her feeling unsettled.

"Yes, he saw me standing by my car and stopped. Otherwise, I might've been stranded there all night." Penny laughed, trying to lighten the mood. But then she caught Stella's eye and knew she hadn't fooled her for a second.

Penny hadn't made a secret of her opinion that Clayton had been hard done by, and perhaps needed another chance. She liked the idea she was standing up for someone who couldn't defend himself. She was righting a perceived wrong. She'd spoken to Stella about it on more than one occasion, saying Clayton wasn't the bad guy everyone was making him out to be. And now Stella was looking at her with a knowing gleam in her eyes.

"I've heard he's good-looking," Stella said, sitting on the edge of her single bed, facing Penny. Clayton had disappeared by the time Stella started working at Stargazer, and therefore only had other people's descriptions to go on. But that didn't stop her from digging for information.

"Yes, he is," Penny finally agreed. She looked up and met Stella's inquiring gaze. Lifting the corner of her mouth, she gave a cheeky smile. "Very good-looking, in fact."

"Ooh." Stella rubbed her hands together and sat farther forward on the bed. "Tell me more." Her French accent became more pronounced whenever Stella got excited. Penny knew that Wyatt, especially, adored her accent.

"There's nothing to tell. He was a friend helping me, that's all," Penny replied, frowning slightly. Well, there was a lot to tell, but not about the topic Stella thought they were discussing. Should she tell Stella what'd really happened tonight? She'd already opened up to Clayton. It'd felt good, too. Cathartic. Not nearly as embarrassing or shameful as she'd imagined. She'd been keeping Mitch and his appalling treatment a secret for so long now, it had become a habit, ingrained in her psyche.

Perhaps it was time.

How would her friend respond to her news? She hoped she knew Stella well enough to anticipate her response; she'd been nothing but supportive so far, a ray of sunshine. They'd shared so much over the past year. She was like a second sister to Penny.

Stella opened her mouth to speak, but Penny held up her hand. "Actually, I have something to tell you, but it's not what you think."

"Go on." There was a mischievous twinkle in the other woman's eye. She was still hoping for more info on Clayton. This was harder than Penny thought. At least when she'd opened up to Clayton, she'd been half-tanked on whiskey.

"I've told no one here. But I was married before."

The twinkle left Stella's eyes, her mouth forming a perfect *O* of surprise.

Penny went on before she chickened out. "I never told anyone because I left him, ran away. He was…" How did she put this? "…a controlling asshole who ruined my life."

"Oh, *chérie*." Stella lay a comforting hand on her arm. The human touch offered a reassurance and commiseration that sent a stab of sadness through Penny. "I didn't know." There was no blame in her friend's eyes for not telling her sooner, just genuine sympathy.

Goddammit, now tears were welling in her eyes. She didn't want to cry, this wasn't what this was supposed to be about. She drew in a deep breath, past the lump blocking her throat, and began to speak, spilling out all the sordid details of her mangled marriage.

This time felt different to when she'd told Clayton. With

him it'd been more of the bare facts, enough to convince him that Mitch was a tyrannical, controlling psychopath. But she found herself telling Stella more of the intimate details. How it made her feel in that first year, when she kept trying to explain his minor faults as mere idiosyncrasies, something she'd have to learn to live with. And then when she'd come to that final decision, which had left her utterly devastated for days. That her marriage was at an end. She couldn't make it work, no matter how hard she tried. That her husband was a monster who wanted to suck the very marrow from her bones, her soul from her body.

Finally, she wept, held in Stella's arms as they curled up together on her single bed. In a strange way, the tears felt good. Raw and real.

Her tears ultimately dried up and she and Stella sat side by side on her bed, the only sound the odd sniffle from Penny.

"So, what are you going to do?" Stella asked the very question Penny couldn't answer.

"I don't know." She pulled another tissue from the box beside her bed and blew her nose. "Those few seconds after he drove away, my only thought was to get as far away from Stevensville as possible. I was ready to leap into my car and go, not even bother to come back to the ranch for my stuff. But then…"

"What?" Stella prompted.

"Then I had time to calm down, when Clayton took me to his house. He said I should go to the cops, not let Mitch scare me out of town."

"He could be right." Stella patted her hand gently. "I don't want you to leave. Of course, if you have to go, then you should go. But I agree with Clayton. Maybe it's time to stand up to your ex-husband, show him he can't scare you anymore."

Penny pursed her lips. "Perhaps," she mused. The same

thoughts had been rolling around in her head while she'd been lying on her bed before Stella arrived. She liked it here. Liked her job, liked the ranch lifestyle, loved the people. Had finally begun to discover her true self again. Could see herself staying here long term. Why should she let Mitch drive her away from this place? He didn't have the right to control her life anymore. If she left, that's exactly what she'd be giving him.

"I can't leave tonight, anyway, my car is still in town," she said.

"True." Stella glanced at her, green eyes worried. "Does that mean you'll stay, at least for Cat and Levi's wedding?"

The wedding was only four days away. And there was still so much left to do; she didn't want to leave her friends in the lurch. Being a part of the wedding was a dream come true for Penny. Cat and Levi were made for each other. It'd be a confirmation that true love was real, as long as you found the right person. Would four days make a difference? If she kept her head down and stayed on the ranch, didn't go back into town, surely Mitch wouldn't dare approach her here? She was surrounded by friends and guests. It'd give her time to plan a proper retreat, if that's what she needed to do. Or at least say goodbye to everyone and come up with an excuse to move on.

Penny finally nodded, and Stella gave a squeal of joy and hugged her. "I'm so happy." Then her mood sobered. "You should tell Naomi. I think she wouldn't judge you, and she might know how to help. At least you would have us looking out for you. How do you say it, we'd have your back?"

"Yes, that's correct," Penny giggled. "That would be nice, to have people who had my back," she agreed. "You're right, it's time I told Naomi. Told more people. This shouldn't have to be my dirty little secret anymore."

"You'll go to her tomorrow, then?"

"I will. But I need to tell her in my own time. Do you promise not to say anything until I'm ready?" It was the same promise she'd elicited from Clayton a few hours earlier.

"Yes, of course," Stella agreed. "Now it's time to go to sleep." She wriggled out of Penny's bed and went to brush her teeth.

She was making progress, she'd told two people her story today, it was an enormous leap of faith. Now, she had to find the right time to tell her boss. Naomi was the best employer in the world, but Penny was still hesitant, wondering how she'd take it. She'd find the courage to tell her tomorrow. And she'd also find the courage to go in and visit Deputy Wilder and file a complaint against Mitch.

Tomorrow was going to be a completely different day. Tomorrow, Penny would take charge of her own destiny.

CHAPTER SIX

Clayton swore and slammed the truck into first gear. Of course, today, of all days, he was having problems reversing the delivery truck. He was attempting to back it up the steep incline next to the last cabin in the row, but there was a sharp bend halfway up, where he had to swing the rear bed around so it didn't collide with the recently constructed front porch. It was a tight space, but normally he could handle this kind of thing blindfolded.

His sweaty palms weren't the result of his bad driving; they were a result of being back on Stargazer land again. George had asked for a huge favor. Their normal delivery driver was off sick this morning. And Todd, the other yard hand, was stuck out on a job, handling a customer complaint about a wrong timber order. So, could he please, *please* drive this load for him? George knew of Clayton's history with Stargazer, and he had never asked him to do a delivery out here before, but he was left with no other option. This was the last load of timber needed for the builders to complete the front porches on all three new cabins for the staff to move into.

Clayton swore again and then drew in a deep breath. *Calm down.* He could do this. Finish the delivery and get going. In and out as quickly as possible. God, he hoped Cat wasn't anywhere near the site. The last thing he needed was to run into her. He wouldn't have a clue what to say. It'd be awkward as hell, and Cat would probably give him a dose of her sharp tongue. Which he would deserve.

Nearly as bad would be to run into Dean, his old boss.

He finally got the truck reversing in the right direction, one of the builders whistling to let him know he was good to stop at the top. Clayton banged his Stetson onto his head and hopped out to undo the tension straps and get this lumber unloaded.

And ran straight into Dean.

Clayton backpedaled a few steps, unable to hide the shock he knew must be showing on his face.

"Good morning, Clayton." Dean didn't give his normal jovial smile, but he wasn't scowling, either. Was that a good thing? Or a bad thing? Clayton couldn't read what was going on behind his ex-boss's eyes.

"Ah…morning, Dean." Clayton tipped his hat, watching Dean warily, still not sure where this was going.

"You working for Butterby's now?" Dean raised an inquisitive eyebrow.

"Ah…yes, sir." The words tumbled out of his mouth before he could stop them. "Penny helped me get the job after I was released."

He wanted to slap his forehead. What a fool. Now he'd probably dropped Penny in the shit as well.

"Did she now?" The other eyebrow went up in surprise.

Clayton wanted to yell at the sky in frustration. This day was getting better by the minute. Not. Shit, he hoped he hadn't just got Penny fired. If he could only take those words back.

"Penny's an excellent woman. Does a great job at reception. I've always valued her opinions highly." Dean ran a speculative gaze up and down Clayton. "And it's good to see you've found a decent job. Got back on the straight and narrow."

It was Clayton's turn to furrow his brow in surprise. Dean wasn't condemning him, wasn't demanding he get off his property and never come back, as he'd half expected. But then, Dean had always been a great boss, understanding and patient, cared deeply about all his staff. Except when he'd believed the worst of Clayton.

There were so many things Clayton wanted to say to his ex-boss. How devastated he'd been that Dean could presume Clayton was capable of doing some of the things he'd been accused of. How much he wanted his old job back; to be a part of this amazing team Dean had assembled, more like a family than staff. And how much he wished for Dean's forgiveness. So much so, it was like a cancer on his soul.

"Look, Dean… I want to say how sorry I am. Things got out of hand, and well…"

Dean waved the rest of Clayton's attempted apology away. "How about we let bygones be bygones? I believe everyone deserves a second chance. Now, do you need a hand getting this timber unloaded? I'm so looking forward to these cabins being finished." Dean called over to two of the builders to come and help before Clayton had a chance to answer.

"Good luck, Clayton," he said over his shoulder as he strolled away.

Clayton stared after him for a few seconds, before a builder tapped him on the shoulder and said, "Are you gonna help us untie this stuff?"

"Sure." Clayton scuttled up onto the truck and released the ratcheting straps. The timber was unloaded, and Clayton hopped in the truck without coming across anyone else from the ranch. Which could only be a good thing; he didn't think he could take another confrontation. Even if Dean had seemed to accept Clayton's apology.

He knew all the dirt roads on the ranch like the back of his hand. Now that he had an empty truck, he could use the service road to get back to the highway without fear of it getting stuck in a rut. The back road wound him through the western side of the property, skirting around the back of five guest cabins. Thankfully, his hands had stopped shaking now. He liked Dean, had once respected him as a boss. Until Dean —along with everyone else—had turned their backs on him. How could they have believed he was capable of arson? Of burning down a cabin? Levi's house? Their betrayal still hurt, like a sore not fully healed. But now, it seemed Dean might've changed his mind. He was always a reasonable person.

Something caught his attention out of the corner of his eye. Hang on. Was that…? Clayton stopped the truck abruptly and a cloud of dust flew up from the wheels. He peered out the window to a cabin now in his side mirror. That had been a white rental car parked in the driveway back there. A white rental car that looked suspiciously like the same one Mitch had been driving yesterday. Was it too much of a coincidence? How many white rentals were there in Stevensville?

Clayton should just keep driving. It was none of his business.

He pummelled the steering wheel a few times in frustration. Damn it, he was going back. He just couldn't leave well-enough alone. He put the truck in park and jumped down. The vehicle would be fine here for five minutes while he went to investigate.

Clayton walked around the front of the building to check on the car. It was definitely the same make and model as the one from yesterday. One of the golf carts used by the staff and guests to get around the property was also parked by in the driveway.

He jogged up the front steps onto the little porch. What was he going to say if the guy actually answered the door? If it was the ex, he could at least let Penny know that the slime ball was on the property, so she could be on her guard. Hopefully she'd decided to go to the cops first thing this morning.

He raised a hand to knock on the door, but an indistinct thump from inside made him pause. There was obviously someone home. What was that noise? There was another thump, accompanied by a muffled scream. Something was going on inside.

It took him two seconds to decide to barge his way through the door. If it was something innocent, then he'd apologize profusely afterwards.

The door was unlocked. He pushed it open and was confronted with a shocking scene.

Mitch was standing in the living room.

And he had Penny by the throat. She was clawing at his hands, trying to wrench them free.

"You will come with me this time, you little bitch," Mitch whispered menacingly in her ear.

"Hey," Clayton shouted. "What the fuck do you think you're doing?" He rushed across the room toward them, and Mitch let Penny go, dropping her like a hot potato, then quickly dodging behind the sofa.

"You again," Mitch howled. "How the fuck…?"

Clayton's first impulse was to grab Mitch by the throat, give him some of his own medicine. Then Penny moaned at his feet and he bent down to lift her into a sitting position.

"Get out of here, you have no right to be here." The other man advanced around the sofa, fists raised like a boxer, eyes full of rage, as if intending to come at Clayton. *Bring it on, asswipe.* Clayton stood up to his full height and stepped over Penny, so she was behind him. Perhaps it was the look of raw anger on Clayton's face, or perhaps the idiot had second thoughts, because Mitch hesitated, fists still raised.

"Come on, big fella," Clayton taunted. "I dare you to take a swing. I want you to take a swing," he growled. At that, Mitch took another two steps away.

"I'll report you to the police, this is breaking and entering," the ex blustered, but there was a sulky tilt to his mouth that indicated he was conceding defeat, albeit ungracefully.

Clayton snorted. Watching Mitch out of the corner of his eye, he bent down again to Penny. "Are you okay?"

She stared at him, eyes as large as a frightened fawn, her breath coming in rasps.

"No. He tried to…" she stopped and gasped in a few painful breaths. "Can you please get me out of here?"

"You bet." Clayton didn't wait to see if Penny could stand, he scooped her up and headed for the door, keeping one eye fixed on the asshole. "We're going straight to the cops," he said to the man still glowering from behind the sofa. He wanted to say that Mitch better run far, and he better run fast, because Clayton was going to make sure Jude didn't let him get away with this latest attack. But this slime ball would most likely hightail it out of here the minute they left.

He carried Penny up the hill to where his truck was parked, then gently slid her into the passenger seat. With one last glance backward—the bastard was nowhere to be seen— he jumped in and took off in a cloud of dust. He pulled his cell out of his back pocket and put it in the cradle on the dash, then began thumbing through his contacts while keeping an eye on the winding road.

"What are you doing?"

"I'm calling Dean, to see if he can stop your ex from leaving the property."

"Oh God, please don't involve them. I still haven't told Naomi. Or Dean."

Clayton could hardly contain his exasperation. "Penny, you can't let him get away with it this time."

"I know," she said so quietly, he almost missed it.

"They need to know what kind of asshole they have staying on the property. It's not fair on Dean if you don't tell them." His finger hovered above the call button.

"Okay," she finally agreed.

Relieved, Clayton made the call. Naomi answered from the front desk, barely hiding her surprise that it was Clayton calling. He gave her the bare details, saying there was a potential criminal staying in cabin thirteen, and asked if she could send a couple of the guys down to check it out, and to detain the man if he was still there. And to watch out, he may be dangerous.

"I've also got Penny with me," he said into the shocked silence as Naomi digested his words on the other end of the phone. "She's going to call you and fill you in on all the details soon. But at the moment, all you need to know is that she's safe."

This time Naomi's silence was more than just shocked, Clayton could feel a heavy suspicion at his words. "Can I speak to her?" she asked sharply.

"Go ahead, you're on speaker," Clayton answered tightly.

"I'm fine, Naomi." Penny paused. "It's a complicated story, and I'm sorry I haven't mentioned anything before. But that guy in cabin thirteen is my ex-husband, and he just tried to hurt me."

"Oh, baby girl," Naomi crooned, "don't you worry, we'll take care of him. Are you..." Clayton hated the hesitation in Naomi's voice, the distrust clear. "...okay? With Clayton, I mean?"

Clayton ground his teeth together, and Penny flicked him an apologetic gaze.

"Yes, everything is fine. He helped me. Like you said, I'll

call you soon."

"Right after we've been to the sheriff's office," Clayton interjected.

Penny glared at him across the bench seat. But eventually she nodded mutely, the distress on her face was hard for him to watch. He couldn't understand why she was hesitant to report it to the police, it was crazy, but she must have her own reasons. The bruises on her neck were turning purple already, and every now and then she fluttered her hands up to her neck, as if still feeling his fingers clasped around it. Clayton almost turned the truck around. He needed to go and beat the living shit out of that guy. The only reason he'd left him standing was because he was worried about Penny, wanted to get her away from there as fast as possible.

Naomi rang off, so she could contact Dale and Big Tom to go straight to Mitch's cabin. But Clayton doubted they'd find him there.

They drove in silence until he turned the truck onto the main highway.

"How did he find you out here?" Clayton asked gently.

"I don't know. But he must've come straight here after... the incident at the florist. He didn't leave town, like he said he was going to."

"Yeah, well, neither of us really believed that bullshit, did we?"

"No," she agreed.

"I didn't know he was staying at the ranch. He must've used a false name. Naomi told me we had a walk-in last night, a man who booked for three nights, but I thought nothing of it at the time. He was lucky to get a cabin; we're usually full at this time of the year, plus we've got the wedding coming up. Anyway, a call came in this morning, a guy complaining that his welcome basket was missing." Clayton cocked his head. His puzzlement must've showed in his frown, because she said, "About a year ago, I suggested we start a welcome pack for all our guests. It's a basket full of local goodies, jams, nuts, cookies, a bottle of wine, that kind of thing. I order the baskets and make sure they're stocked in each room before a guest arrives. Anyhow, I thought the pack may well have been missing, because the guy had arrived late last night, while I was still at your place, and so no one would've thought to take it down for him."

Comprehension was dawning on Clayton. That clever son of a bitch.

"I said I'd take him one directly."

"Of course, you did," he replied.

"It never even crossed my mind that Mitch would try something like this, that he'd do something so sneaky and underhanded. I really underestimated him."

"Yeah, well, we won't underestimate him again."

Penny shot him an odd look, and he suddenly realized what he'd said. He'd used the word *we*. It'd been automatic, because he felt like he needed to help her. Perhaps he'd overstepped the boundaries.

"I'll drop the delivery truck back at Butterby's; it's on the way. We can take my pickup to see Jude," he said, returning his gaze to the road, fixing on what was important right now.

"Okay." She looked so small and shrunken, huddled in the seat beside him. Her black Stargazer T-shirt was still rucked up from where he'd carried her out of the cabin, exposing creamy flesh at the top of her jeans. But she also looked different somehow. Then it hit him.

"You're not wearing your glasses."

"They fell off in the scuffle." She gave him a peculiar, sideways glance. "I'll let you in on a little secret. I don't actually need glasses; they were part of my disguise."

"Oh, right." That sexy librarian disguise, boy that turned him on. "That's a good thing though, isn't it? At least you can still see." His voice was light, joking almost. But inside, he was seething. Penny had gone to so much trouble to change her whole look, to disguise herself so that Mitch wouldn't locate her. She was such a vibrant, energetic woman, and yet she'd been forced to stoop to this. But it'd all been to no avail, because he found her anyway.

He stole a quick glance. How would this end for her? Would she be able to go on with her life the way it was? Unchanged and unaffected? Somehow, he doubted it.

CHAPTER SEVEN

Deputy Wilder stared at Penny from across the desk. "Clayton tells me you're having a problem with your ex-husband."

"Technically, he's still my husband. He never signed the divorce papers," she replied, picking at the edge of the table, not meeting the deputy's gaze.

"That shouldn't make any difference. He'll still be charged with assault. Going by the bruises on your neck," Jude tilted his chin in her direction, "I'm assuming you want to press charges?"

Penny glanced at Clayton. No, not really. She just wanted to forget this all happened, pack her stuff into her car and move on. Go to a better place. A safer place, where he wouldn't find her.

Clayton stared back at her, his ice-blue eyes steady, a calming influence on her crazy thoughts.

"Yes," she murmured. "I do."

"Give me a second to dig out the paperwork on his restraining order, and I'll set things in motion." Jude stood up and left the interview room.

"You're doing the right thing," Clayton said, as soon as Jude exited.

"I know," she agreed. "But it's hard. I can't explain it. Maybe I just don't want any of this to be real. If it was all a dream, then…"

"Yeah, well, life doesn't always go the way we planned it," he replied, a cynical tilt to his gorgeous mouth.

She winced, reminded how much Clayton's life had changed in the past few years through circumstances over which he had no control. Much like hers.

Before she could say anything more, the deputy came back into the room. "I've got the paperwork. I've also dispatched Deputy Nomad to Stargazer to see if we can track this man down."

"You won't find him at the ranch," Clayton growled. "I already told you, Dale and Tom said the cabin was abandoned by the time they got there."

"We have to start somewhere," Jude said levelly. But it made Penny's skin crawl, to think that Mitch was already three steps ahead of the police. That he was out there somewhere, perhaps looking for her again. Hopefully, he was hightailing it home, like the coward he was, not waiting for the police to catch up to him and face what he'd done.

Jude cleared his throat in a way that made Penny turn her head to look at him fully. "I, ah…also heard some…worrying news." His brown eyes softened, gaze moving from Penny to Clayton and then back to her. "Deputy Nomad mentioned we've had a report of a car torched in a parking lot last night."

Sharp claws clutched suddenly at her chest and she found it difficult to breathe. An icy slither of foreboding slid down her spine. No, it couldn't be.

"What was your vehicle registration?" Jude asked gently.

"Oh no," she said in a whisper. "He wouldn't. Would he?"

She gave Jude her license plate, and he confirmed it'd been her car they found. His confirmation hit her like a jackhammer, and she clutched at her chest to try to stop the ache forming behind her breastbone.

"That's so…violent. Mitch was never that audacious. This just seems so petty. Beyond him, somehow."

"Well, we don't know for sure it was him," Jude replied. "It could be some kids playing a prank."

Penny frowned at the deputy. "How likely is that?"

Jude shrugged and said, "It's possible."

"But it's more likely to be her ex," Clayton interjected.

"Yes," Jude agreed. "And if it is, it may mean he's escalating. You said he wasn't normally violent toward you."

Penny nodded.

"And now, in the space of two days, he's tried to physically abduct you twice, as well as allegedly set your car ablaze. In my experience, we need to be careful when an offender's crimes intensify, as his seem to be. We need to take this seriously."

The news that her car was gone sent her thoughts spiraling downward, and she only half listened to Jude.

"What am I going to do? I've got no vehicle now. No way of escaping." Her last words came out more as a wail. The emotions churning around in her stomach were too much to hold down. Feeling suddenly trapped, she stood up in a rush. "I can't stay here." Her gaze darted around the room looking for something, anything to get her out of here. "I need to leave; I can't breathe in here."

Clayton materialized by her elbow, his warm hand steadying and solid in the small of her back. "It's all right," Clayton said gently.

Jude stood as well and faced her across the table. "If you give me a few hours, I'll see what I can come up with. We might be able to catch this guy before he crosses the state line. And if not, we can at least trace where he's been. Hopefully, he's left the state."

"Why don't you come back to my place?" Clayton's hand was still in the small of her back, holding her like she was a fragile piece of bone china, about to break. "We can wait there. Jude can contact us, and let us know as soon as they have any info on Mitch." Her hands were shaking, and all she knew was she needed to be out of this room, away from the four walls that were closing in on her. "I'm assuming those bruises on her neck should be all the ammunition you need to hold this bastard for at least a couple of nights if you catch him?" Clayton's last question was directed at Jude.

"We certainly will hold him until formal charges can be laid, if we find him," Jude replied.

Clayton's touch had a calming effect, soothing the rising panic in Penny's belly, and her mind cleared enough for her to grasp the meaning of his words and understand what he was suggesting. Clayton was going to look after her. He was putting himself out again to protect her.

"Aren't you supposed to be at work?" she asked.

"Yes, but that's easily fixed. I'll tell George I have a family emergency. He won't argue with that." Clayton waved away her worries.

He would do that for her? Take a day off work. Take her back to his place, provide her with a safe haven.

"I'm asking too much of you," she said flatly, backing away, releasing his hand from her back.

"No, you're not. I need to know you're safe. I need to see this through to the end." Clayton took hold of her hand, pressing his thumb over the soft rise of her wrist, his blue eyes imploring.

She lowered her gaze. "I'm sorry, I should never have gotten you involved."

"I chose to become involved when I stopped my pickup. It wasn't your decision to make," he retorted.

She wanted to ask him why he was doing this. Was he

looking for some kind of redemption? Would helping her somehow absolve him of his sins? Or was he doing this out of kindness, a version of friendship? But she didn't want to go back to the ranch. There'd be too many people asking too many questions. Questions she couldn't face at the moment. She hated to leave Naomi in the lurch because they were so busy right now, what with Cat's wedding coming up. As of Friday, all the normal summer guests would check out, leaving room for Cat and Levi's family and friends to stay, which was at least a little less stressful. But she couldn't return to work today. Not feeling the way she did. Funnily enough, she'd felt safe at Clayton's last night, and she knew she'd feel safe there again today. It'd be nice to have a calm place to sit and sort out her feelings, regroup and decide what to do next.

"All right, but only for a while," she finally agreed.

"Good." He let go of her hand, but the hard line between his eyes softened slightly when she agreed.

"Before you go." Jude held up a hand, but the look on his face was one she couldn't decipher. He pursed his lips and then gave a small grimace. "Sorry, Clayton, this is going to sound bad, but I have a duty of care to make sure Penny is safe. Don't take this personally."

Clayton took a step back and crossed his arms, his face hardening slightly. "Go ahead," he said. "I know what you're going to say."

Jude's tone took on a serious note that made Penny frown in dismay. What was he on about? "Penny, I need to make sure you're going willingly with Clayton."

"Of course I am. Why would you ask that?" She glanced at Clayton, but his gaze remained fixed out the window, his blue eyes hard.

"I assume you know about Clayton's history. With the ranch, and his conviction for abduction and assault."

Realization suddenly dawned. She was putting Clayton in an awkward position simply by being with him. Because people still distrusted him. Her agitation turned to anger. All he was trying to do was help her.

"Yes," she replied coolly. "I know everything. And I'm not bothered by his…past at all." She went over and laid a hand on Clayton's arm. The tension running through him was palpable.

"That's good." Jude expelled a breath of relief. "Because Clayton served his time and so he is free to go about his business in the community. But I wouldn't be doing my job properly if I let you go with him, without understanding his history."

"Thank you," she replied, leaving her hand where it was, showing Jude in no uncertain terms where her loyalties lay.

Clayton's features softened, and he looked down at her.

"He has every right to say this," he murmured.

She wanted to shake her head and tell him that Jude should keep his thoughts to himself. But instead, she said, "Shall we go?"

"Yes, I just need a quick word with Jude here. Do you mind waiting in the hallway for me? I'll only be a few minutes."

"Sure." She was surprised that he wanted to talk to Jude after that, but she backed out into the hallway, and leaned against the wall, staring through the open door, watching Clayton while he talked quietly, but urgently to the deputy.

Today, Clayton was wearing a body-hugging, black tee and jeans. He'd left his white Stetson and plaid shirt in his pickup. The outfit was simple, with obviously little thought put into it. But the effect on her hormones was something else altogether. She could see the planes of his shoulder blades outlined beneath the soft fabric, traced the veins running down his bicep, watched those tanned forearms and the capable hands as he gestured to make a point. He was one hell of a hunk of man. And in this second, when she allowed herself the pleasure of outlining his broad shoulders, down to where his jeans sat low on lean hips, her mouth began to water.

She needed to stop daydreaming. Refocusing her awareness, she leaned in and caught snatches of Clayton's conversation. "…two men at the warehouse… they were gone when George… I'm worried…"

That got her attention. What was he worried about?

It was Jude's turn to speak. "…overreacting… pending court case…FBI say that…" Then Jude shook his head. "Leave it with me and…" She took a few stealthy steps forward, to try and hear more, when Clayton suddenly turned to leave the room. She sprang backward and attempted to appear as if she was nonchalantly leaning against the wall. Was Clayton in some kind of trouble?

"Make sure you go straight to Clayton's house and stay there. I'll contact you as soon as I have any information." Jude shook Clayton's hand and gave her a serious nod. Jude was a well-respected deputy in this county, and had a reputation for being solid and dependable, good at his job and good at protecting the people of Stevensville. She trusted him to get it right, more than she trusted the police back in Santa Barbara. At least here, she was more than just a name on a bit of paper. Here, she was a part of the community, rather than one more crazy housewife seeking a restraining order on her husband.

Clayton's house was only a ten-minute drive from the sheriff's office.

"I'll make us a coffee," Clayton offered as he pulled up in the driveway. "Harry will be at work all day, so we've got the house to ourselves."

What, no whiskey today, she wanted to quip, but she kept quiet. Instead, she watched him move around, collecting the makings for the coffee, his body almost too big for the cramped kitchen. Last night, she hadn't stopped to think that she'd been alone in the house with Clayton. But today, things felt different. Now, she was aware of his every move, aware of the way his gaze hovered on her, then flicked away. As if he was just as aware of her.

"How you take your coffee?"

"Cream and sugar, please."

He placed the mug in front of her and pulled out a seat opposite, the move reminiscent of exactly what he'd done last night. She nodded her thanks, and they sat in silence, sipping their coffee. His sky-blue eyes watched her above the rim of the mug. Then he stretched out his long legs beneath the table and their shins collided. The shock of the contact almost had Penny's coffee slopping over. When she glanced up at him, there was heat in his gaze that hadn't been there earlier. Or had she just missed it? The room suddenly seemed too small, as tension hovered around them. She licked her lips, an unconscious move, but it drew his gaze to her mouth, where it rested. The intensity of his stare made her cheeks flame hot.

Back when Clayton was working at the ranch, Penny had allowed herself the odd fantasy, indulging herself by wondering how it would feel if Clayton kissed her. Would his kisses be full of passion and determination? Taking her mouth, claiming it as his own?

After he was accused of the arson attacks, Penny's daydreams had gone up in a puff of smoke, so to speak, and she'd never indulged again.

But now…? Those fanciful wishes came back to haunt her.

What would it feel like to kiss Clayton?

"You should call Naomi, let her know what's going on."

"What?" Holy cow, how could she be daydreaming about those kinds of things when her life was going down the toilet?

"I will, in a minute," she promised, giving herself a mental shake. Naomi would most likely be going crazy with worry about her; she thought of her staff as family, and worried about each and every one of them. "But first, you need to tell me what your conversation with Jude was all about."

Clayton sat back in his chair, the furrowed line back between his brows. He took another sip of his coffee while he studied her.

"I'm not sure that's any of your business." His gaze was dark now, boring into her, his countenance unreadable. But she wasn't giving up that easily.

"Perhaps not. But you're all up in my business now, whether I like it or not, so fair's fair." When he remained glaring at her, she added, "I need to know if you're putting me in any danger."

At that, he gave a deep, loud laugh, and she winced as the irony of her statement hit her.

"I think it's the other way round, lady," he said, waggling his eyebrows. He put his coffee mug down and fixed her with his stare.

"Well," she huffed. "Then maybe I can help protect you. I'm not completely useless, you know."

"I'm sure you're not—"

Penny didn't let him finish. He might've rescued her twice in the past twenty-four hours, but he needed to know she had some skills at self-preservation. "I'm damn good at throwing a knife. I took a class, about a year before I left Mitch. I told him I was learning circus skills. He thought it was juggling or something. I needed something to make me feel in control, like I had some power over my own life..." She stopped, suddenly embarrassed by her boasting tone.

Clayton held his hands in the air in mock surrender. "I'm impressed," he said. She studied him for a second to make sure he wasn't actually ridiculing her. She was pretty sure he meant what he'd said. "It's good to have defensive skills. I mean it. That's not an ability I expected…"

"A woman to have," she finished for him with a smile. "I only stopped because I left Mitch." It was a shame she'd let her expertise fall by the wayside. Perhaps she'd take it up again, soon.

"All right, I'll tell you. But you need to keep this to yourself."

"You won't find many people better at keeping secrets than me," she replied cynically. A sad but true statement about her life over the past few years.

"You remember, around six months ago, when Wyatt and Stella got involved with that diamond heist? And they ended up running through the mountains to get away from the mobster who wanted the gems back?"

How could she forget? Stella was her best friend; she'd been worried sick about her safety. "Of course, I do. But that whole horrible episode ended well, didn't it?" As far as she knew, Wyatt and Stella were now safe. Tony, the guy who brought all the trouble down on them, was dead, as were the two other men who tried to take Cat and Levi hostage.

"You might think it's over, but the reality is, the guy who was pulling the strings from in jail, Dmytro, is still running the show as if nothing happened. The police want to nail him for murder and trading in stolen diamonds on the black market. They want to get this bastard."

"What does that have to do with you?"

"I want to get this bastard, too. While I was in jail, I had a few dealings with him. I know things about him and his thugs. So, when I heard that Stella and Wyatt had been forced to go into hiding, I wanted to do something to help. I went and told Jude what I knew."

Penny watched Clayton talk. He was a paradox. Here he was, going out of his way to help Stella and the cops. And yet, he had this dubious background, had done so many things wrong, but was still trying to claw back some form of normality for himself. Now he was helping her, too. She had to respect that. Even though life had dealt him terrible blows, and even though he'd become jaded by it, he still wanted to do the right thing.

"The FBI are trying to talk me into going on the witness stand."

Penny pursed her lips. "Wouldn't that put you in danger?" If this Dmytro was as bad as Clayton was implying, and he could control his gang members from inside prison, then Clayton needed to watch his back.

"Maybe," he said, the dark frown back. "Which is why no one else can know."

Clayton stared at her casually, sipping his coffee, but she got the distinct feeling he wasn't telling her everything.

CHAPTER EIGHT

Should he tell her about the two men at the warehouse yesterday? He didn't want to scare her. And Jude had downplayed his worries, saying it was highly unlikely they were Dmytro's men. The mob boss was under lock and key, and tightened security. The way Jude put it, the guy couldn't even fart without a prison guard knowing about it.

Clayton decided to keep it to himself, for now.

"I won't tell anyone about your links to Dmytro, I promise."

He knew he could trust her; that wasn't his problem. His problem was he shouldn't be involving her at all. But it felt good to confide in her. Apart from a few people at the sheriff's office, the two FBI agents, a lawyer, and Harry, Clayton hadn't told anyone else what he was doing. Penny was the first friend he'd told. The thought hit him like a brick to the side of his head. That was because Penny was the only friend he had. Which was a sad reflection of what his life had become.

Enough of his own wallowing in self-pity, time to change the subject.

"Shouldn't you call—?"

"Just about to." Penny waved her cell at him.

Clayton got up and began tidying the coffee mugs away while Penny made her call. Even though he could only hear her side of it, he could tell Naomi was upset and worried about Penny. At one point, Penny swiped at a tear, as her eyes welled up over Naomi's sympathy. Naomi wanted her to come back to the ranch, thought she'd be safer there. Penny softly but firmly disagreed with her, saying she would stay at Clayton's, at least until they heard something from the sheriff's office.

Penny hung up and sat staring contemplatively out the window. He let her be. It was nearly lunchtime. He opened the refrigerator and stared at the scant contents. What on earth could he make her to eat? He finally settled on a grilled cheese sandwich, and got out the last of the bread and a hunk of cheese. He gave it a surreptitious sniff. It still smelled decent. Then he turned on the stove and began to butter the bread.

"Do you think I should call my family?" she asked.

Her question took him by surprise.

"I'm probably not the best person to ask. I don't have a good history of strong family connections." He grimaced.

She stared at him, her ocean-blue eyes bleak, and he relented a little. "You said your sister knows what Mitch was up to. What about your parents?"

"I tried to tell my mom a few times, but she always explained Mitch's behavior away, saying that was normal in any marriage, you had to expect minor bumps in the road. It got to the stage that I stopped saying anything." Penny tugged gently on her braid as she spoke; he'd noticed it was a habit of hers when she was thinking aloud. "I called and told them I'd left him; I even told them why. My dad wanted to go over and, in his words, *teach him a lesson*. He wanted me to move back in with them. But all my mom said was that a bit of time on my own might do me some good."

"Ouch." What a bitch. He didn't say that out loud, however, as Penny probably wouldn't appreciate him calling her mother out. Clayton moved back to the table, pulling out a chair and sitting down, giving Penny his full attention.

"My mother has never been overly affectionate," Penny continued. But Clayton saw through her flippancy, to the deep pain her mother's lack of warmth had caused. At least his mother was supportive; maybe Penny's had missed out on the mothering gene. It seemed her parents were the polar opposite to his. It was his father who'd reacted badly to his prison sentence. Yet, her father wanted to stand by her. It was the mother keeping her at a distance.

"Going back to live with my parents was never an option. Mitch would never leave me alone if I did that. I knew I had to make a clean break and get away from everyone. So, I agreed with my mother, told a little white lie, and said I'd been offered a fantastic job up in Washington state. That's where they think I am right now. I call them every month, do the dutiful-daughter thing to let them know I'm okay." Her words slipped out softly, but he could hear the sad regret in her tone.

"Wow," Clayton breathed. His life suddenly didn't seem so shitty. Her parents didn't even care enough to even keep tabs on her; they weren't actually aware of where their daughter was. When Penny had first started working at the ranch, she'd seemed very reserved and withdrawn. He put it down to her being naturally shy, but now he could see how scared and worried she'd been. If only he'd known from the start, perhaps he could've done something to help. But then again, perhaps he couldn't. These were her choices, and she probably wouldn't have done anything differently.

Without thinking, he reached across the table to lay his hand on top of hers. She stiffened slightly, then gave him a wan smile. She looked so lost, so forlorn. He wanted to see that pretty smile again. Families were difficult, he knew that much. And there was no way he could change her family dynamics. But he could offer her moral support.

"I'm worried that Mitch might target them; use them as a way to get to me, now that he knows where I am," she continued, her beautiful mouth drawn down in a sad pout.

Clayton didn't disagree with that assessment. From what he'd seen, this Mitch guy was a loose cannon, capable of anything. "You should call them and warn them, then."

His thumb traced back and forth across her knuckles. Her skin was so soft. Unlike his work-hardened hands, covered in cuts and calluses. She tipped her head to the side, her braid falling off her shoulder as she regarded him. Eyes the color of a rainy ocean considered him. Large eyes that drew him in. He could make out small scatterings of gold and silver flecks in their depths. It was nice to be able to gaze directly into her eyes; she looked better without her glasses. Her gaze flicked down to his lips and then shot up again, as if catching herself in the act. That slight movement fired a shot of heat into his guts.

"Hmm, maybe I should," she replied absently, her lips parting slightly on the words.

He moved closer, drawn in, a puppet on a string, dancing to the yearning he could see in her eyes. Two years ago, he'd wondered what it'd feel like to claim her lips. Wondered what she tasted like. That old urge grew a hundred-fold as she sat across the table from him. The air around them crackled with tension. It was as if he were frozen in time, unable to move, except toward Penny. She was the only thing in this room that mattered.

He had to kiss her. There was no alternative.

Unsure who moved first—perhaps they both leaned across the table at the same time—his mouth found hers. Not soft and tentative, but firm and challenging.

She made a noise in the back of her throat, as if savoring something sweet and delicious. The sound soon turned into a growl; one of possession, of hunger. Her other hand came up to his cheek, pulling him closer, letting him know she wanted this as much as he wanted her.

He needed to get closer, the table was in the way. Pushing his chair back without releasing her lips, he shoved the table sideways. She came with him as they stood together. Her hand left his cheek and wound around the back of his neck. Then she was hard up against his chest; he could feel the glorious, round softness of her breasts against his ribs. Her black Stargazer T-shirt hugged her figure nicely, sitting right on the waistband of her jeans, giving him a tantalizing feel of pale skin against his fingers every so often.

While she wasn't short, he still had to lean down to reach her lips. She would be the perfect height to fit neatly under his arm. She reached up, tilting her head to allow him the best access to her mouth. One hand ran down over her perfect butt, pulling her in even closer, so her hips were wedged in between his. His body became a burning ember, her touch igniting all the nerve-endings in his skin. Her nimble fingers reached up underneath his T-shirt, finding the bare skin beneath, her fingernails digging in slightly, raking them down his back.

The smell of scorching grease reached his nose. He ignored it. Even if the house was on fire, he couldn't drag himself away from this woman. Her kiss was like heaven. Like salvation.

But Penny must've smelled it, too, because she finally pulled back far enough so she could look him in the eye. "Is something burning?"

"It could be me," he replied with a lift of his mouth.

"No, really. Is something burning?"

"I turned the stove on. It's just smoking a little." He was

half hoping they could ignore it and go back to their delicious interlude, but her fingers withdrew from his waist and she pushed gently against him. With a sigh, Clayton extricated himself from Penny's arms. Damn, he'd been enjoying that. More than enjoying it, he was getting lost in her. The way he hadn't gotten lost in a woman in a very long time.

"Sit down and I'll make us a grilled cheese sandwich," he said, thinking he did a grand job of keeping the regret out of his voice.

Penny stepped out of his arms, the look on her face hard to decipher. Did she regret kissing him? Because he didn't regret kissing her. Perhaps it was a stupid thing to do. The last thing either of them needed was another complication in their lives. But it also made him feel more alive than he had in the past few months. Scratch that. In the past few years.

"Thank you, that would be nice. I missed breakfast this morning," Penny said, taking a seat once more at the table. As she moved to sit, the bruising on her neck caught his eye. A flicker of shame crawled through his guts. How could he be thinking of kissing her, after what that bastard ex-husband had done to her? He felt her eyes on him as he moved around the kitchen, preparing their lunch, and he wondered what she was thinking. He wanted to say something, to break the nervous silence that'd descended, but she beat him to it.

"I'm going to call my sister while you get lunch ready. I might step outside, if that's okay?"

"Sure," he replied. "Go out on the back porch if you like. I'll bring the sandwiches out when they're ready." He pointed toward the back door. There was an old table and chairs out there, with a nice view over the large, unfenced property, with the Bitterroot Mountains as a backdrop. He often sat out there, contemplating life. The house might be old and in desperate need of TLC, but like most places in the valley, it had a view to die for.

"Thank you."

He watched her slip out the back door, couldn't help but notice her hips swaying nicely in those blue jeans.

Five minutes later, Clayton shoved the door open with his knee, balancing two plates and two glasses of water in his hands.

"Lunch is served," he called.

But Penny wasn't sitting at the table, as he expected. She was standing on the bottom step, staring out over the pasture, a frown marring her beautiful face.

"What's the matter?" Perhaps she'd seen a wild deer, they often came through here. Although, not usually in the middle of the day.

"I saw a man. Over there." She lifted a hand and pointed toward a copse of apple trees on the edge of the property, left over from when the place had been part of an orchard.

That had Clayton's attention. "Are you sure?" he snapped, senses suddenly on full alert.

"Yes, I'm sure. Look there's two of them now."

Clayton shaded his eyes, looking in the direction Penny was pointing. It was a fair distance, around two hundred and fifty yards. He glimpsed movement, then two figures broke from the trees and began to run toward them, sprinting across the long grass of the pasture. Holy shit. Whoever those men were, they didn't look friendly. He needed to get Penny out of here. Now.

CHAPTER NINE

"Quick, inside." Clayton grabbed Penny by the arm and towed her through the back door, slamming it behind him and locking it. She wanted to say he was hurting her, but she caught his urgency and held her tongue.

"Let's go. Out to the front. Get in my truck," he commanded.

Okay, now he needed to give her something more. Those men running toward the house had looked scary, like they were up to no good. But surely, they were safe in the house, weren't they?

"What's going on?" she demanded. She knew her face was full of shocked disbelief as she stood, staring at him, phone still clutched tight in one hand from where she'd hung up on her sister.

"I'll tell you when we're in my truck. Get going." Jesus, he sounded just like her dad when he was in one of his moods, ordering her around. When she still hesitated, he said, "We don't have time for this." The genuine fear in Clayton's voice finally got to her.

He followed her to the hall, and they went out the front door—he didn't bother locking this one—down the steps and were in the truck in ten seconds flat, Clayton almost bodily hauling her up into the cab, and Penny doing exactly as she was told, biting back the million questions crowding her brain.

It wasn't until after he backed out of the driveway and he was driving safely down the road she finally asked, "Who were those men? Why were they spying on the house? Why are we running away?"

"I'm sorry I yelled at you," he said. But his attention flicked from her to the rearview mirror as he scanned the neighborhood, and she understood he was still worried. "They're all good questions; none of which I have an answer for. I don't know who they were," he said, and she could hear the truth in his tone. But there was also something else, something he wasn't telling her. As they sped away from the house, she let her gaze scour the area as well, not sure what she was looking for. There was a black sedan parked down the alleyway between Clayton's house and the one next door. Did that car belong to the neighbors? She didn't remember seeing it when they arrived.

Then Clayton pulled the truck around a sharp corner so fast, Penny had to grab for the handrail. He was in a hurry, as if he was still expecting a pursuit.

Her mind scrambled to understand what was happening. She grasped at the only feasible solution.

"So, if you have no idea who they were, is it possible that could've been Mitch? Maybe he's found himself an accomplice. Maybe they've come for me?" Her voice pitched up high, and her chin wobbled.

Without taking his eyes from the road, he replied, "It's a possibility. I didn't get a good look at the two men running towards us, did you?"

"No, sorry." And Clayton hadn't given her time to wait around to find out.

"They did both have a similar build to Mitch," Clayton

mused. "But so does about half the male population of Montana."

Clayton didn't have any enemies, so it made more sense if it were Mitch coming for her. Although, that wasn't completely true. Hadn't he just told her he was perhaps going to be a star witness in the trial against a vicious mob boss?

Before she could voice her concerns, Clayton swore.

"Shit." He was staring in his rearview mirror.

She turned to peer through the back window, and saw a car coming up fast behind them. The same black sedan that'd been in the alleyway. There was a sound, like something pinging off metal. Were they shooting at them?

"Duck your head," he yelled and yanked the steering wheel, weaving the truck all over the road. She bent at the waist and got as close to the floor as possible, resisting the urge to cover her ears and scream like a little girl. Clayton's house was on the outskirts of Stevensville. It was a small town, and out here, there were semi-rural properties as far as the eye could see. But soon, they'd be heading to suburbia, surrounded by houses and shops. Surely, the men behind them wouldn't shoot in a built-up area?

"Are they shooting? Like real bullets?" Her question came out as a squeak, and she wasn't sure if Clayton heard.

"Yes, stay down." Clayton gripped the steering wheel with hands clenched so tight his knuckles went white. More bullets pinged off the bed of the truck. Holy shit. What should she do? She'd never been shot at before. She wanted to yell at Clayton to duck down as well, because he was now a prime target. The thought of a bullet slamming through the truck and into the back of his head made her want to vomit. The pickup screeched around another corner and she felt it lean over, almost on two wheels. She was impressed at his Formula One driving skills. Taking a chance, she glanced quickly in the side mirror. Even with his radical driving, the other car was catching up to them.

"Where are we going?" Penny yelled, her words muffled slightly as she kept her head below the dash. They needed an escape plan; they couldn't keep driving around like this forever.

"There's only one place I know where these thugs won't follow us," he replied grimly. "To the sheriff's office."

It was a brilliant idea; at least one of them was still thinking logically. Lifting her head quickly, she saw more houses appear, then Clayton slammed the pickup around another sharp bend at the last moment, probably hoping to throw the sedan off their tail. Penny hit her head as the truck lurched and gave a loud whimper.

"Sorry," Clayton said.

"Don't apologize, drive faster," she replied.

Another glance showed houses crowding in on both sides, the wide country road becoming narrow and well maintained, the front yards tidier. She knew where she was; Main Street was only two blocks away. But a glance in the side mirror told her the black car had gained on them, and was now almost hitting the rear bumper. They were still shooting, but now, instead of bouncing harmlessly off the back of the truck, the bullets were embedding in the cab's roof. One smashed through the rear window, and Penny screamed. Shit, that was too close for comfort.

Suddenly Clayton demanded, "Sit up straight and hold on tight."

She shot him a confused look but did as he asked. Why would he put her in more danger? Clayton floored the gas pedal, and the truck jumped ahead of the sedan.

"Hold on." She saw him cross his fingers on the steering wheel, then he slammed on the brakes. There was a loud crunch, and they were both thrown forward as the sedan slammed into the rear bed of Clayton's truck. The seatbelt bit into Penny's shoulders and hip bones, but it saved her from any more harm.

Clayton put his foot on the pedal again and they roared away, leaving the sedan smoking in the middle of the street, its front end a crumpled mess.

"I think that worked," she said. He'd shaken them off, hopefully given them enough breathing space to make it to the sheriff's office.

But right before they turned onto Main Street, she saw the sedan begin to roll down the road behind them, still in pursuit, the front bumper dragging on the ground and steam pouring from the engine.

"They're coming again." Her warning was more of a loud groan.

"I see them." Ignoring the speed limit, Clayton drove as fast as he was able, overtaking other cars in his way, aiming to get to the other end of Main Street before the sedan caught up.

The car was gaining, but the traffic hindered them, too. They rounded the bend at the end of Main Street and drove the next block at breakneck speed until the courthouse and sheriff's office came into view. Clayton screeched into the curved driveway of the building, the front wheels bouncing up the curb.

"Come on, they won't dare follow us inside." He came around and made sure Penny was out of the truck safely, then he took her hand and they bounded up the front steps of the county building.

Jude met them at the front door. "We just got reports of shots fired out on Baldwin Road. Was that you?"

"Yes, someone's chasing us. Shooting at us from a car," Clayton panted, pushing past the deputy. "Let us in, I need to get Penny safely inside." They both stood in the foyer to catch their breath, as Jude stood in the doorway and scanned the area. Penny could've told him the other car was long gone; it peeled away around the corner a block away, clearly recognizing where they were headed. Jude scrutinized Clayton's parking effort and the damage to his truck before he closed the door, but said nothing.

"Give me a description of the vehicle," the deputy demanded. Penny stayed quiet while Clayton gave him a quick account of what happened. There was a flurry of activity as Jude organized Deputy Nomad and their deputy trainee to go out and look for the car. He made a few calls to the police in Missoula, also asking them to be on the lookout. It shouldn't be too hard to find a black sedan with a crumpled front end.

"Come into the interview room and we'll get the details." Jude ushered them down the hallway, and Penny remembered the room well. She could hardly believe it was only this morning she'd been in here. "Take a seat, the sheriff will want to be in on this, I'll get him," Jude said.

They sat quietly, both too shocked to speak. Clayton reached out and took her hand, blowing out a loud breath.

The sheriff bustled into the room, closely followed by Jude.

"Twice in one day. Don't tell me you're causing more trouble." Penny couldn't believe they were the first words out of the sheriff's mouth. Suddenly, Penny got a first-hand view of what Clayton had to deal with on a day-to-day basis. The sheriff knew Clayton was innocent, and yet even he still judged him. She caught Jude's raised eyebrow in the sheriff's direction. At least Clayton had one person on his side.

Clayton just shook his head, looking tired.

Sheriff Buchanan sat down, stroking his impressive mustache thoughtfully. The sheriff could be abrupt and overbearing, but he always kept the best interest of the community at heart. Penny knew Cat didn't like the sheriff, and had locked horns with him more than once, especially over the case of whether Clayton had been innocent. But Penny was reserving her judgement on the large man in front of her.

"Did you get a good look at either of these guy's faces?" Jude asked, also sitting, a pad and paper at the ready to take down notes.

They shook their heads in unison. "Sorry, we were too busy ducking bullets," Clayton growled.

Jude pursed his lips. Penny knew it wasn't ideal, and the story might even sound far-fetched, but they believed them, didn't they?

"Go over the whole thing from start to finish. Give us as much detail as you can," Jude requested.

Clayton recounted from the time he stepped onto the back veranda, until the minute they came through the county building's doors, with Penny filling in any bits she thought he missed. Jude's frown deepened with every word, and he was the one who prompted them for more details when they finished their tale. Penny couldn't tell if the sheriff's occasional grunt was that of encouragement or disbelief. She hoped they were taking them seriously. After what'd happened with Stella and Wyatt, how could they not?

"It seems you both have opposing views as to who these alleged gunmen might be," Jude finally said.

She glanced at Clayton. His blue eyes were shadowed, devoid of emotion, as if he'd shut down, no longer able to think. She knew how he felt, this was all too surreal. But perhaps for Clayton, this was all too *real*. After all, he'd been here before, and the cops hadn't believed him then.

"Which do you think is the more likely scenario?" Penny asked, deciding to take the lead.

"I agree with Clayton's theory. It fits with the two guys he saw at the warehouse the other day."

Penny gave Clayton a stony-faced look, and he lifted a

corner of his mouth as if in apology. "I should've told you. I thought I was protecting you."

So, this wasn't just two random guys attacking them for no reason. This Dmytro guy really was a threat. She still wasn't a hundred percent sure this didn't have something to do with Mitch, but she kept quiet.

Penny checked her phone; they'd been talking to Jude for half an hour already. As if picking up on her agitation, Jude said, "We've had a couple of cruisers scour the whole town. There's no sign of a damaged black sedan."

"Are you surprised?" Clayton asked, running a hand tiredly across his eyes.

"Not really," Jude replied.

"What do we do now?" Penny asked the question they were both thinking. "We can't very well go back to Clayton's house." Should they perhaps go out to the ranch? Would it be any safer there? Penny didn't want to involve Dean and Naomi. Not unless she absolutely had to. This wasn't their problem; definitely not their fight. And Dean might not welcome Clayton on his property. Poor Clayton, he didn't need that kind of rejection. What kind of person would she be, if she took shelter at the ranch and left Clayton to the mercies of those gunmen? He hadn't left her when she needed help, and she would not leave him in the lurch, either.

Clayton sat straighter in his chair. "What about a safe house? Do you have somewhere we can go?"

Laughter erupted from Sheriff Buchanan, his mustache bristling with mirth. "A safe house? Here? In Stevensville? Who the hell do you think you're kidding?"

Penny tensed at his words. There was no need to be so rude.

"I think what Hank means," Jude interjected, "is that we're a small office in a small town. We don't have those kinds of facilities here. The FBI might be able to help you. They could have a safe house in Missoula. Did you want me to ask them? Be warned, if I do that, things will get a whole lot more complicated." Jude shot her a quick glance. "And they might only offer protection for you, not Penny. They may not see that she's connected to Dmytro and therefore assume she's not in any danger."

Clayton shook his head emphatically. "No. The less I have to do with those guys, the better. And we need a place where both of us can go."

Penny wondered what he had against the FBI. Surely, that was the safest place for him right now. She knew nothing about the internal workings of the infamous Bureau, only what she'd seen and heard on TV, which was bound to be wrong. Maybe it was as simple as Clayton not wanting this to escalate; wanting to keep it in-house, if possible. Or maybe he was looking out for her. Did she want his protection? Perhaps Jude was right; if these guys really wanted Clayton, then if she left him, she'd be safe.

Sheriff Buchanan stood, lifting his impressive bulk slowly out of the chair. "I'll leave you in the deputy's capable hands. Let me know what they decide." The sheriff tapped the table in front of Jude.

"Yes, sir."

They all waited until Hank left the room. Penny decided that Jude was wasted here. He was young, eager, dedicated and invested in helping them. Unlike the sheriff. He would go far one day.

Jude leaned across the desk. "Personally, I think it'd be safer if you two stayed together. At least, for the next little while. We haven't been able to locate your ex-husband, which means he could still be in town." Jude hesitated. "There's also a possibility those guys saw Penny, know who she is. She might be considered a target, as well."

That was interesting, the fact Jude wanted them to stay

together. It told her he still was unconvinced this whole shootout didn't have something to do with Mitch, and he was playing it safe. Funnily, his prediction that she might be a target for mobsters didn't scare her nearly as much as it should. Jude wanted to keep all his eggs in one basket, and Penny could understand that reasoning.

"I might have a place you can stay," Jude said, raising a conspiratorial eyebrow. "It's nothing official, it belongs to a friend of a friend. He uses it as a fishing shack, down by the river. It's pretty basic, but no one would find you there, I'd be the only person who knew where you were."

"What do you think?" Clayton turned his blue eyes to look at her.

Did he realize he was asking her if she wanted to hide out in a shack somewhere isolated, alone with him?

CHAPTER TEN

Clayton zeroed in on Penny, hoping to find the answer in the blue depths of her eyes. He knew he was asking a lot of her. Hell, this was one crazy scenario. He regretted not telling her about the two men at the warehouse earlier. Because if he'd done that right from the start, warned her off him, she may have stayed away. It was the guys from the warehouse who'd been shooting at them, there was no doubt in his head. They must've found out where he lived. And he'd inadvertently dropped Penny in even more trouble. She didn't need this. Didn't deserve this.

Penny blew out a breath and leaned back in the chair. "Do I have a choice?"

He wanted to say, *of course you do*, but he also wanted to keep her safe; wanted her with him so he knew unequivocally that she was protected. Which was a conflicting phrase. Because her remaining by his side could possibly be the most dangerous place for her. The bruises on her neck reminded him of how much danger she could be in. But Dmytro's men were a lot scarier than Mitch. If they got hold of Penny… He stopped his thoughts from going there, it wouldn't help anyone.

"I guess it can't hurt for a day. It gets me out of sight, in case Mitch is still hanging around," she said thoughtfully. "But only on one condition."

Both Jude and Clayton froze. Conditions were never a good thing, especially coming from a woman who'd been pretty much backed into a corner.

"I know this probably isn't on your radar right now. But Cat and Levi's wedding is coming up in a few days. I'm one of her bridesmaids."

Shit, she was right, he'd completely forgotten about the wedding. The chances of her attending that now were low, but he plastered a smile on his face, not giving anything away.

"I really want to be there for her. I need to call her and let her know what's going on," Penny continued.

Clayton glanced at Jude. "That's probably not a good idea, protocol sa—"

"Are you really going to spout protocol at me?" She stood and glared at Jude over the desk. Clayton silently willed Jude to shut up. If they were going to convince her to do this, she needed some leeway. "I don't expect you to understand what it means, to be someone's bridesmaid. But it's a pretty special job, not half of it involving running all kinds of last-minute errands for the bride. I hate to let her down."

Clayton knew enough about women and weddings to understand that this was a huge thing for her to have to give up. Even while her life was on the line, she was still worried about how the wedding would turn out.

"I'm sure this will be over soon," Clayton said soothingly. "We can't have you missing the wedding of the decade. Everyone in town is talking about it."

But Penny wasn't listening, instead she tapped her finger on her lips, her eyes glazing over as if suddenly deep in thought. "Hell, I'll have to talk to Stella, too. I'll need to ask her if she can go to the cake tasting. And someone needs to take delivery of the chairs for the glade ceremony. Maybe I should call Emily. Oh, shit, I need to tell Naomi what's going on, as well." Penny looked up. "Can I borrow your pad and a pen? I need to make some notes on what else has to be done."

Jude tore a sheet of paper from his pad and handed it to her, along with his pen. Penny had slipped into her no-fuss, super-professional attitude she always wore when she was working the reception desk at the ranch, and she didn't notice his slight air of incredulity. But Clayton knew that she, Cat, Stella, and Emily were a close-knit team; he could understand her not wanting to let her friends down.

"Okay, okay." Jude raised his hands in the air. "You have five minutes to make your calls. Use the phone at the front desk. Not your cell. But try to keep the number of people you call to a minimum. And don't, under any circumstances, tell anyone where you're going." This last statement was delivered along with a flat stare. When Penny merely nodded, more focused on her growing to-do list, he cleared his throat loudly. "I mean it, Penny. Both Clayton's and your lives depend on it."

She stopped what she was doing and glanced up at Clayton as understanding grew in her eyes. "I get it," she said finally, her gaze not leaving his face. "I'll make it short and sweet." She went back to her writing and Jude left the room, so only Clayton heard her mumble, "God, they're all going to hate me."

Ten minutes later, Clayton's pickup was parked in the county compound, out of sight and out of reach, and they were heading north out of town in Jude's personal car—he said the cruiser was too conspicuous. Clayton had asked Jude to give Harry the head's up on what was going on, too. To let him know to keep an eye out. But he should be safe, now that Clayton was out of sight, there was no way anyone would mistake Harry for Clayton.

They drove in silence, Jude continuously glancing in his rear-view mirror, and it made Clayton jumpy to realize he was keeping an eye out in case they were being followed. Penny sat quietly in the back seat, staring out at the passing scenery. Making those phone calls had upset her. She kept it well-hidden behind her smile and in the flurry of activity to get them ready to go to the cabin. But her pretty, blue-green eyes were full of melancholy. It must be hard for her; she clearly took her responsibilities seriously. To have to let her friends down like that was driving a dagger deep into her compassionate heart. And it was all his doing. He wanted to punch something, but instead took a deep breath and turned his gaze outside the car.

He never tired of this view. It was one of the reasons he'd come back here after his release from jail. The blue summer sky went on and on and on. Today, a few feathery clouds sat atop St Mary's Peak. Snowdrifts often remained high on the saddles of the mountain all-year round. But this summer had been exceptionally hot, and the peak was now completely barren, rising like a jagged tooth toward the heavens. Stargazer Ranch had the perfect position; situated in a small valley running off the main Bitterroot Valley, it was nestled in the foothills of the mountains. If only he could own a property like that; wake up to a view like that every morning, make a living off the land, then life might be almost perfect.

Jude turned the car onto a secondary road, and Clayton concentrated on where they were headed.

"Can you look at those directions I wrote on that piece of paper?" Jude pointed to the center dash. "I've never been here before. Sam gave me directions over the phone."

Clayton picked up Jude's hurriedly scribbled map and tried to decipher it. By the looks of it, this cabin really was isolated. If it was as close to the river as the map suggested, it might be a nice place to stay. Picturesque, even.

But twenty minutes later, when they pulled up in front of the small, wood cabin, Clayton decided that maybe picturesque wasn't the right word. This was no luxurious, Stargazer Ranch cabin. He made a face at Jude that he hoped Penny wouldn't see. Then he placed his Stetson carefully on his head and exited the car.

"I know this isn't the Hilton," Jude called over the roof of his car. "But it's all I've got. Sam assures me the cabin is well stocked and should be clean enough. He only used it a few weekends ago."

Clayton opened the rear door for Penny, and she stepped out, brows lowered as she assessed their new accommodation. "I wasn't expecting the Hilton," she replied, at last. "This will do."

Tall Douglas-firs crowded in on the small clearing, making it almost cool, the heavy shade keeping the worst of the afternoon heat at bay. Clayton could hear the river gurgling over rocks and glimpsed the bright glint of sunlight off the water around a hundred yards away. The surroundings were pretty as a picture. If the circumstances were different, Clayton wouldn't mind staying in this spot at all.

"Shall we check out the inside?"

They had nothing, apart from the clothes on their backs. Jude promised he'd return later tonight with some supplies. Clayton was hoping there'd at least be the basics, like canned food and matches to start a fire.

"Sure." Penny let them lead the way up the two steps onto the small front porch. Her passive acceptance of the whole situation was making the hairs on the back of his neck stand up. He didn't like this dispassionate acquiescence. He wanted the lively, enthusiastic Penny back. Would she be like this the whole time they stayed here?

It suddenly hit him. He was about to be cooped up with Penny Smith, in a cabin in the woods for the next few days.

Alone. Together. After that scorching kiss in his kitchen today, he hoped he'd be able to control his libido.

Jude foraged around beneath the stairs and came up with a small metal box. "Sam leaves the key here." He passed it over for Clayton to open the front door. Clayton was about to usher Penny in front of him, when he thought better of it. "I'll go first, in case there're any critters in there."

She recoiled and let him past. The interior was a pleasant surprise. The place wasn't nearly as basic as Clayton had been expecting. The cabin was a single room, but it'd been divided neatly into sections. A large, double bed hunkered in the corner—the heavy, wooden frame looked like it might've been handmade—with a curtain that could be drawn across the corner for privacy. There was a well-designed little kitchenette in the opposite corner, with a gas stove and a small refrigerator. Four chairs sat around a round, wooden table, and a brightly patterned sofa filled the last corner. A heavy-duty rug that covered most of the floor completed the decor. A door behind the table led off to what Clayton assumed was the bathroom. It was snug and cozy. Clean and well-maintained. Jude must've been erring on the side of caution when he said it was basic. Penny might even like it.

Scanning the room quickly for wildlife, he called out, "It's safe to come in."

"Wow, this is nice." Jude sauntered into the middle of the room. "Much better than Sam made it out to be."

Both men held their breath as they waited for Penny's reaction.

"It is kind of charming," she said, doing a slow turn. Then she sat on the sofa and stared out the large, picture window. Clayton glanced at Jude and back at Penny. These next few days might be harder than he originally hoped.

"Sam said you're welcome to go fishing, the rods are in the storage shed around the side. The key for the shed is on that hook over by the fridge." Jude pointed to the kitchen corner. "There's all kinds of hunting gear in there, as well. Rope, tackle boxes, buckets, knives. I think there may even be a bow and arrow. And there's a scaling and gutting area down by the river. Personally, I'd recommend you stay indoors and out of sight as much as possible. Electricity comes via a generator, in the same shed. But again, I'd advise you not to run it at night if possible, and leave all the lights off, that way, you're not advertising your presence."

Clayton nodded along at Jude's advice. Was Penny even listening to Jude's instructions?

"Oh, I nearly forgot. The hot water system is under the floor, so the pipes don't freeze in winter. It's run by the generator, but if you need to access it for any reason, there's a hatch in the floor in the bathroom. I think Sam uses that area for storage in the winter, as well."

Clayton filed all that information away. He'd go exploring later on to see if there was anything that might be useful. Useful for what, he had no idea. Because they had no idea what they were up against. Were those men going to keep coming for him? Or had they been scared off when he went straight to the cops?

"Right, I need to get back to work. I'll see you both tonight. Hopefully, I'll have some good news, and you can both go home." Jude stopped with his hand on the door. Penny didn't react; it was as if she hadn't heard him.

"That'd be great." Clayton followed Jude out onto the front porch. "I'm sorry I haven't said this before, but thank you, Jude. You've gone above and beyond the call of duty here."

"All good." Jude waved away his gratitude. "Besides, this is purely selfish," he added. "I don't want another episode like that with Wyatt and Stella happening in our county. We've had enough gang-related deaths in our little town to last a lifetime."

"Ah." Clayton hadn't thought of it that way. Jude was doing his job, protecting the innocent in the best way he knew how.

"She seems a little…shell-shocked." Jude said as he placed his brown sheriff hat thoughtfully back on his head.

"Yeah, nothing has gone according to plan for her today. I'm hoping she gets over it soon." It was true. Clayton felt sorry for Penny, her whole life had been turned upside down in the space of twenty-four hours. It was no wonder she'd gone semi-comatose.

"Hmm. It might be a quiet few days," Jude replied. "Remember not to turn your cells on." He got back into his car and Clayton watched the dust rise as he drove up the dirt track. It was the only way in or out of the place.

Peace descended once the purr of the engine disappeared. Birds sang in the trees. A fragile breeze tickled the pine needles, making the branches sigh. Dappled sunlight filtered through the tree limbs, casting a crazy pattern on the cleared earth around him. The sky was so blue and big above the treetops. Montana was often called Big Sky Country and with good reason. The big sky had a certain quality about it. A sharp brightness that lifted the soul.

Clayton took his first deep breath of the day. Really breathed in the clean air, tinged with the smell of the river not too far away.

Things might work out, after all.

He leapt up the front steps, feeling lighter than he had all day. If he could pull Penny out of her funk, then all the better.

He opened the door to find her standing in the middle of the rug, eyes wide and apprehensive.

"I think I made a mistake coming here. I need to leave." Penny pulled her cell out of her back pocket and stared at it. "I'm going to call Jude to come back and get me."

What in hell was he going to do now?

CHAPTER ELEVEN

Penny stalked back and forth across the pebbly beach by the river, arms crossed over her chest. The moment Jude had disappeared up the road, the enormity of what was happening to her and Clayton came down on her like a ton of bricks. She didn't want to be here. Didn't want the pressure of the lurking danger threatening to blow her mind. Didn't want to think about men with guns shooting at their car. Didn't want to think about Mitch with his hands around her throat. She wanted to be back at Stargazer Ranch, getting ready for Cat's wedding. It was in three days' time. How could she possibly not be there to support her friend? It was unthinkable.

Clayton had talked her out of calling Jude, reminding her what Jude had said about keeping their cells turned off, and asking her to give it an hour before she let anxiety overwhelm her. His smooth, baritone voice had taken the edge off her panic, cleared away some of the fog of the building hysteria. But she couldn't stay in the tiny cabin, so she told Clayton she was going for a walk. His lips thinned, but he said nothing, just gave a curt nod.

She knew he was watching her from beneath the shadows of the large pine tree farther up the bank, even though she'd told him to leave her alone; that she needed her space. He was worried about her, but that didn't make her feel any better. She was as jittery as a frog on a string, feeling like she'd been suddenly put in a cage with no way out. Which was ridiculous, because she was standing out here by the fast-flowing Bitterroot River surrounded by virgin forest in a place so beautiful her heart should be aching.

In truth, her heart was aching, but not because of the beauty around her. It was aching because it felt like there was a rock sitting in the middle of her chest.

Part of the problem was the sudden realization at just how close she and Clayton were going to be. The cabin was small, with hardly any privacy. Everything about this day had heightened her senses. Including her awareness of Clayton. It felt like her skin itched every time Clayton was in the same room as her. There'd been a few times, even as they sat in Jude's office, where she found her fingers reaching out of their own accord, wanting to touch him. Feel those strong, firm muscles beneath her hands. Feel the warm flesh of his tanned forearms.

How was she going to resist him while they were locked together in this isolated hideaway?

She'd made this decision willingly; she hadn't been coerced or forced. So why was she suddenly backtracking?

There was a hint of movement up at the tree where Clayton was hiding. He was getting agitated, she could tell. How long had she been down by the river, pacing back and forth like a caged lion? She went to pull the phone out of pocket and swore, remembering that it was turned off. One more restriction that was chaffing at her sanity. She lifted the phone, wanting to throw it in the river, but stopped herself just in time.

"Penny, are you okay?" Clayton stepped forward into the late afternoon sunlight, concern written all over his face. She didn't want to go back to the cabin. Not just yet. And she didn't want to look into Clayton's blue eyes, because she'd lose it, she just knew she would. Tucking the phone back in the pocket, she scrambled over the rocks, hoping to get across to the other side of the river.

"I'm fine," she called out. "I just need a little more time." She could see a little grassy dell on the other side. It looked like a wonderful spot to sit and get herself together.

"Jude said we shouldn't spend too much time out in the open," he reminded her.

But Penny was beyond caring. Turning her back on him, she faced the river, plotting out a route where she could jump from rock to rock to get across. There was a large boulder a few feet away. If she leapt up onto that, then there was a pile of jumbled river rocks that would take her halfway into the river. From there it looked like an easy task to pick her away across a raft of steppingstones, as the water swirled into a large shallow bend. She wondered if the man who owned this shack had perhaps laid some stones to create a makeshift crossing.

She bent her knees and tensed, ready to launch herself over to the large boulder.

"Penny, what—"

Clayton's voice pulled her focus just as her foot landed on top of the boulder. Her ankle buckled beneath her and she fell to her knees, scrabbling to grab a hold with her hands. But it was too late, and she fell backward into the river with a splash.

Cold water closed over her head, but it wasn't deep. Her backside hit the river bottom, and she bounced up, finding herself in chest deep water. As she regained her feet, pain speared through her ankle and she screamed.

Water streamed off her and she blinked, trying to focus, feeling around blindly with her hands for something to grab hold of.

"Penny." Clayton was suddenly there in the water with her, lifting her up. Then he had her in his arms and was striding up the riverbank. He settled her gently on the stony beach.

"Are you okay? Are you hurt?"

"My ankle," she gasped, brushing water from her face.

"Is that all? You didn't hit your head?"

Penny shook her head.

"Let's get you up to the cabin. I'll look at your ankle there."

He lifted her up again before she had time to argue. His arms were strong and warm around her, even if his clothes were soaking and cold, just like hers. The only silver lining in this whole thing was her phone was waterproof. But was Clayton's? Had he just ruined his cell by jumping into the river to save her?

She gave into being carried by Clayton like a wounded bird and lay her head on his chest, embracing the shelter of his arms. A sob broke from her throat. A hot, fat tear rolled down her cheek, and then another. Oh shit, she was crying. How the hell had that happened? To make things worse, her teeth began to chatter. Was it from the cold water—even in summer the Bitterroot River was never warm—or was it reaction setting in?

She didn't notice when Clayton carried her through the front door of the cabin; she was crying so hard. It wasn't until he placed her gently on the sofa she realized they were inside.

"I…I'm s…sorry," she moaned through her sobs. "I…I don't k…know why I'm crying."

"I do," he replied, brushing a lock of wet hair away from her face. "You've had a shit of a day."

"But I don't normally cry," she wailed. And then buried her head on his shoulder as he took her into his arms. The tears wouldn't stop, flowing freely down her face as she wept like never before.

"It's a form of release," he whispered. "It's all right, I'm scared, too. You'll be okay. We both will." His last comment sounded like he was reassuring himself as much as her. It was true, it did feel like a dam was breaking inside her. All that pent-up emotion from the terrifying events of the day, mixed in with the fear she was going to miss Cat's wedding. All that time and energy spent planning it, and now right when everyone needed her the most, she was abandoning them. It was all too much.

How long they sat there like that she didn't know, but eventually the burdensome feeling subsided, the great weight in her chest easing. She looked up at Clayton. They were both sitting on the sofa in their soaking wet clothes, dripping on the rug. If she wasn't so sad, it'd be funny. Her ankle throbbed, but she decided it was probably only a sprain.

She pulled back slightly, wiping her tears with the back of her hand. It was in that second, she registered Clayton still had his arms around her. He was watching her, that slight furrow between his eyes smoothing as her eyes met his. Oh God. The corner of his mouth lifted in that cute, crooked smile. Tension suddenly oozed around them. This was exactly what she been afraid of. But now she couldn't turn away.

They stayed like that for moments on end. She was close enough to lean in and take his lips if she wanted to. Electricity crackled between them. God, he was so gorgeous. That stubble covering his chin; she remembered it rasping delightfully over her cheek when they'd kissed earlier. That wonderful straight nose, giving him the look of an ancient warrior. Now he was frowning at her again, blue eyes intense, like an icy fiord.

All emotions fled. Except one. Desire. So strong it threatened to overwhelm her. She wanted Clayton, so badly it hurt. She forgot about her problems, forgot about where they were and why they were here. Her mind centered on the immediate here and now. The other stuff would still be there when they came out the other side of…whatever was about to happen. She could hardly believe she was considering making love with Clayton. But she was.

He was too hard to resist. She leaned in one inch, and then another, and let his mouth collide with hers. Because, for the life of her, she couldn't come up with one single reason not to kiss him. It was meant to be. His mouth fit perfectly against hers. At his first touch, a fire erupted in her belly, settling deep between her legs. His fingers stroked the side of her face as he explored her neck, then the soft spot behind her ear with his mouth, and goosebumps raised up all over her skin. She wanted to melt into a puddle of desire.

Half her problem down at the river had been trying to deny her growing attraction to Clayton. That was part of the reason she'd been freaking out. Now, she knew she was never going to beat this pull; it was too strong. Giving herself the freedom to finally let go was liberating. Excitement and anticipation fizzed through her. They were really going to do this. An attraction that'd been simmering for two years was finally going to come to fruition. Whatever came afterwards, she'd face the consequences then.

"We need to get out of these wet clothes," he growled into her neck.

She couldn't agree more. He'd pulled his T-shirt up and over his head before she had time to do more than blink. Oh. My God. Those abs. Exactly how she'd imagined. Her knees went weak at the sight and she wanted to lick her way down his taut stomach, just to taste his skin. The jeans were a bit more problematic. Cold and wet, they stuck to his thighs. And oh, what impressive thighs they were. All that hard work at the building yard sure had made him fit and well-muscled.

Kneeling carefully on the floor, she helped him off with his shoes and then dragged the hem of the wet pant legs over his heels. When he was completely naked, Clayton stood and let her look her fill. He was so stunning; he had her holding her breath.

Mitch had never been this…dominating. No, that wasn't the right word. Clayton wasn't trying to dominate her. But he oozed a cool self-confidence about his body and about his pure maleness that was such a turn on.

He took her by the hand and helped her up to standing. She'd completely forgotten about her ankle, and when she put weight on it, her leg almost buckled beneath her.

"Ow."

That sexy crooked grin lit up his face, and in one fell swoop, he'd scooped her up and carried her over to the bed in the corner. "I'll look at that right now."

But Penny wasn't thinking of her ankle, the only thought going around her head was that Clayton was completely naked, carrying her to the bed. She wished her clothes would miraculously disappear from her body, so she could feel his glorious skin against hers. On impulse she tugged on her T-shirt, awkwardly dragging it over his head, even as he held her in his arms. Her bra was too difficult to manage, so she left that on. He could take care of that later. He gave a growl of appreciation as her bare skin hit his. Now, that was more like it.

He lay her carefully on the bed, as if she were made of spun glass. She fumbled with the top button of her jeans, but he batted her hand away.

"Let me do it."

Oh God, that mischievous grin was back, setting fire to her insides. She lay back and watched as he knelt down next to the bed and his dexterous fingers undid the buttons, one by one. She'd never felt so aroused by the simple act of a man undoing her pants. Gently, he wiggled the jeans over her hips and slid them down her legs, taking care when he came to her injured ankle.

She raised her head and watched him inspect her foot. Gentle fingers probed the area.

"It's quite swollen," he muttered. "Does it hurt if I do this?" He rotated her foot to the side.

"Ow, yes it does," she huffed.

"What about if I do this?" He moved it up and down.

Surprisingly, that wasn't so bad, and she shook her head. He palpated the joint with his fingertips. She loved watching the concentration on his face. He was so intense, so focused. Then his features split in a smile.

"Good news, it's not broken. Just a sprain. Would you like me to get some ice for you?"

"Not on your life. You're not going anywhere," she said, rising onto her elbows.

"Well, now, from a purely practical point of view, I would advise against that." He winged up an eyebrow. "But, from a purely selfish point of view, I'm liking your style."

He lightly kissed her foot, his gaze never leaving hers. Then he kissed her shin, feathering his fingers up behind her knee. It sent shivers of pure pleasure through her. His lips skated slowly up her leg, planting kisses all the way along, his hands stroking her skin sensuously. He was at her knee, then her thigh, climbing higher and higher. The furnace in her belly, lit by his earlier kisses, became more intense with every inch he climbed. Holy cow, this was exquisite. She was melting.

She should be having second thoughts. It was way too early to be sleeping with Clayton. She'd never done anything like this before. She'd only ever experienced the traditional methods of getting to know a guy. Dating and chocolates and roses worked when you had time on your hands. But then again, these were extenuating circumstances. They'd been through so much together, the past twenty-four hours felt like a lifetime; like she'd known Clayton for an eternity. They were two people experiencing trauma, with troubles dogging them both. Neither of them needed this sort of complication. Neither of them needed to get mixed up in the other's problems. And yet, here they were. Entwined together on a bed in a tiny cabin.

His mouth reached the top of her thigh and then he planted kisses across the fabric of her panties. His fingers lifted the hem and slid slowly, ever so slowly, underneath the silky material, stroking the hair at the juncture of her thighs.

"Lovely as these are, I much prefer the view without them on."

Penny's mouth went dry. Then her panties landed on the floor and all thoughts about taking things slower fled from her mind as his experienced mouth worked over her belly. He elicited feelings she'd never experienced before. Her mind was a pile of mush as her body demanded she fulfill its cravings.

He was on the bed beside her, undoing her bra in a rush, as if he couldn't wait, either.

"Mmm." The sound was more a vibration in his chest. "Gorgeous."

She wanted to say the same thing about him, that he was the most delectable thing she'd ever seen, but her tongue wouldn't work, and her brain lost all capacity to speak. Instead, she hooked her hand around his neck and dragged his mouth down to cover hers.

She wanted to feel the full length of his body against her, and she squirmed beneath him, giving out a small whimper when he didn't immediately obey.

Clayton moved sideways and put a small foil package on the bedside table. She smiled at him. She liked a man who was prepared; he'd put her mind at ease without even having to say a word.

Then he came back, crushing her into the bed as his chest landed on top of hers, lithe hips slotting between hers, legs long and lean down the length of her own, his erection pushing against her stomach, silky and firm. A sigh of unadulterated pleasure left her lips. This was how it was supposed to be. As if she'd been waiting her whole life for this one moment.

She sank into the blissful oblivion of making love to Clayton.

CHATPER TWELVE

The sound of a vehicle had Clayton jumping out of bed. He was shocked to see it was almost dark outside. Shit, he'd completely forgotten Jude was coming back. Quick, he needed to find his clothes.

A few moments later, Clayton tucked his shirt and ran a hand through his hair, before opening the door. Dusk was creeping in around the cabin. He should probably go and start the generator, so they had some light. But it was too late to do it now Jude was here. At least their clothes were mostly dry after their dunking in the river, but his damp jeans had been hard to pull on in his hurry to get to the door.

"Hi, come in," he said, hoping Jude hadn't noticed his quick glance toward the bathroom. Penny was in there getting dressed. He'd carried her over when she tried to leap out of bed and crumpled onto the floor, forgetting all about her swollen ankle. Out of the corner of his eye, he spied a pair of panties on the floor, next to the bed. Damn.

Clayton peered out the door before he closed it, noting that Jude had driven the sheriff's cruiser tonight. He shut the door in time to see Jude place an armful of paper bags on the countertop in the small kitchenette.

"Not sure what you needed, but there's all the basics in

there. Milk, bread, fruit, biscuits."

"Thanks. We really appreciate it." He pointed Jude toward the sofa, while he pulled out one of the dining chairs and sat on it.

"Penny's in the bathroom." Clayton waved a vague hand in the direction of the door. Then his tongue seemed to stick to the roof of his mouth, and he couldn't come up with any more sensible conversation, silence crowding around them like a cloak.

"Shall we wait for her to come out?" Jude asked, removing his felt hat and placing it neatly on the side table.

"Hmm? Oh, yes, good idea." Clayton leapt up and busied himself putting the kettle on. "Would you like a coffee?"

"No, thanks." Jude gave him a curious glance, like he knew something was up, and Clayton's heart jumped in his chest. Thankfully, the deputy decided not to ask, because he knew his edginess must be clearly written all over his face. Not that he wouldn't have admitted what he and Penny had just done, if Jude confronted him. But Clayton wasn't ready to tell anyone about it if he didn't have to. It was too real. Too raw. Too surprising. And way too exceptional to share.

"We were…ah, just about to rustle up some dinner. Have you eaten?"

"I'm all good, thanks." Jude took out his small notebook and consulted the pages, while Clayton riffled through the bags Jude had brought, pulling out a packet of dried spaghetti and a jar of Bolognese sauce. That'd do nicely. He lit the gas stove and put a saucepan of water on to boil.

There were a couple of candles in the corner of the countertop. He lit those and transferred one to the dining table where it emitted a soft, enticing light. The silence in the cabin grew loud again.

At last, there was the sound of a toilet flushing, then water running from a tap and Penny finally opened the door. She hobbled out into the main room.

"Oh, Jude, hi." Clayton had to applaud her feigned innocence, but it was probably too late. The look on Jude's face said he suspected them, even if he tried to hide it for Penny's benefit.

Then he noticed her hobbling. "What have you done?" Jude asked, half-standing from the sofa, a concerned frown darkening his handsome face.

"I was rock-hopping, and I fell in the river. Clayton assures me it's only a sprain." She gave him a chaste smile, and it reminded him they still hadn't iced her ankle yet. He found the ice box and wrapped up a handful of ice in a dishrag as she hobbled toward the sofa. Then he pushed another dining chair close, so Penny could rest her foot on it when she sat down. He adjusted the ice pack, so it sat evenly on her ankle, and she gave him a grateful smile.

"That's not good." The frown remained on Jude's face.

"Oh, it should be better in a few days," Penny replied.

"I'll bandage it up to help stop the swelling after we've eaten," Clayton added.

"No, I mean, it's not good to have you incapacitated."

"Why not? I mean, it's not like I need to run a marathon soon, or anything," she joked. "Do I?"

Jude must've seen the growing concern in Penny's eyes, because he seemed to change tack. "No, you're right," he agreed. "Lots of rest, and you should be right as rain in a few days." But the concern still hovered in the way Jude gripped his pen extra tight, and Clayton wondered exactly what the deputy had found out in the couple of hours he'd been away.

"What news have you got for us?" Clayton asked, suddenly worried.

Jude studied them both for a second. "It's not as good as we might hope," he admitted with a grimace. He turned to address Penny. "We still can't track down your ex-husband.

There has been no sign of him since he left the ranch this morning. Apart from his rental car, which was found abandoned opposite the bus depot in town."

Shit, had it really only been this morning that he'd caught Mitch holding Penny by the throat? The day had blurred into one giant rollercoaster. The bruises still clearly evident on Penny's throat should be all the reminder he needed.

Jude went on. "Which could be a good thing, or a bad thing. He doesn't seem to have crossed the state line, unless he's stolen a car. We have alerts out at all the rental companies. We've asked police up in Santa Barbara to monitor his house, so they'll let us know if he returns home. We've checked all the buses and flights out of Missoula, but there's no sign. Unless he's traveling under an alias. Could that be a possibility?" He cocked his head in Penny's direction.

"Anything could be possible. He's changed a lot since I was with him. Become bolder. More desperate." Penny had re-tied her blonde hair into her usual long braid, which she was now tugging on with ever-increasing force.

"Hmm." Jude tapped his upper lip with the end of his pen. "I'm sorry to say, that without a confirmed sighting, we should assume he's still around somewhere. He's still a potential threat."

"Oh, God," Penny whispered, her face losing all color, as the significance of his words struck her. She could be stuck here for days until he was found.

That wasn't the best news, but Clayton wasn't as worried as Penny seemed to be. He could handle Mitch. The man was a bully and a posturer who used fear and his warped sense of self-importance to rule. But Clayton knew he could take him on and win, if it ever came to that. As long as Penny let Clayton stay around, she wouldn't have anything to fear from that asshole.

"Don't worry." He comforted her with a hand on her knee. "I won't let that…him touch you."

She turned to him, eyes wide, tension radiating from her hunched shoulders. But as he squeezed her knee, letting her feel the comfort of his touch, she nodded and sat back in the sofa, seeming to accept his cool observation. She was coming to trust him. As the thought struck him, a sudden pain speared behind his ribcage. People had trusted him once; but not anymore. He'd thrown their trust back in their faces when he'd run away, instead of staying to confront his problems. And afterwards, he doubted he'd ever earn anybody's trust again. But here was Penny. Sweet, courageous, open-hearted Penny, giving him her trust.

The problem was, he didn't know if he deserved it.

"What about Dmytro's men?" He turned back to Jude, leaving his hand on Penny's knee.

Jude glanced astutely at Clayton's hand before saying, "Pretty much the same. Absolutely no sign of them. They've gone to ground. And we're only assuming they're Dmytro's men. This shooting could be completely unrelated."

Clayton gave a loud snort. "Highly unlikely."

"I agree," Jude said with a placating tilt of his head. "But in law enforcement, you learn to keep all options on the table. Stranger things have happened."

Clayton could see the logic behind Jude's words, but he knew in the core of his guts that these guys were Dmytro's thugs. Come to silence him, so he couldn't speak at the trial.

"We have a state-wide alert out for their car, using your description. And forensics is analyzing some of the slugs we dug out of your truck, to see if we can match them with a known weapon."

"But what you're telling us is that we need to sit tight. Wait it out." Clayton sighed. He'd heard it all before. He'd become extremely good at sitting and waiting while he'd been in prison. Waiting to see a lawyer. Waiting for his trial date. Waiting to be acquitted of the arson charges. Then waiting out his six-month prison term for the intended abduction of Cat. All the lawyers and prison guards and even Jude, telling him to be patient, that these things took time. He'd spent over a year in jail, served his time, and finally been set free.

He was getting tired of waiting. But it seemed the only option, and if the truth be known, he was happy to wait if it meant he got to spend more time with Penny. She'd need his help, especially with her injured ankle.

"Got it in one." Jude stood and placed his hat on his head. "Are your cells still turned off?"

Shit, Clayton had completely forgotten about his phone. He hoped it was okay after the dunking in the freezing river. It was supposed to be a waterproof version, but he'd never tested it out.

"Yes," they replied in unison and then grinned at each other with a conspiratorial look.

"Riiiiight." Jude gave them another questioning glance. "I'll be back sometime tomorrow with more updates. Just sit tight, this will all work out in the end."

"I hope so," Penny said. "And I hope you remember that the wedding is only—"

"Three days away. Yes, I haven't forgotten," Jude said, not unkindly.

Clayton showed Jude to the door. "Thanks, Jude, you're going above and beyond. I want you to know we really appreciate it."

"No probs." Jude walked down the steps and disappeared into the dusk. "Remember to lock the door." His voice drifted back from up the driveway.

Should he go and start the generator? It seemed like they didn't need it tonight; it might be nice with the candles. He could always turn it on later, if they needed it, for hot water or to cool the refrigerator.

With Jude's words of warning still ringing his head, he went back inside, attempting to erase any signs of disquiet that might be showing on his face before Penny saw him.

"How does spaghetti Bolognese sound for dinner?"

"It sounds wonderful," Penny replied from her spot on the sofa. "I'm starving."

Now that he thought about it, they hadn't had a chance to eat his grilled cheese sandwiches for lunch. They were still sitting out on the the back porch, where he dropped them when the men with guns had come toward the house.

"I'll do it," he said, holding up a hand, as Penny went to stand up.

"Are you sure?"

"Of course, I'm sure." This was the second time today he'd prepared food for more than just himself. It felt good.

The water was boiling, so he added the spaghetti. Then he found some tomatoes and a head of lettuce in the bags Jude had brought and made a simple salad.

Penny watched him with hooded eyes. "Do you think he suspected?"

Clayton didn't need to ask what she meant.

"Yeah, he knew exactly what we'd been up to."

"Shit." Her exclamation and was quiet but intense.

He wanted to ask her why she was worried. A part of him wanted to take offense Penny didn't need to shout from the rooftops that they'd had sex. That part of him believed she was ashamed of what they'd done. But another, larger part of him understood her reticence. This was new, surprising even him. They'd made no promises. Even though he was desperate to make love to her again, right now. There were so many obstacles in their path, it seemed impossible they could ever find their way through the maze.

He went over to the sofa, leaned down and kissed her on

the lips. The jolt as his mouth brushed hers, alleviated all his fears. She responded to his touch as eagerly and she had an hour before. The passion was still there.

"Don't worry," he said quietly. "Jude won't tell anyone. Our secret is safe."

She exhaled in relief, her breath warm across his cheek. Then she pulled back so she could gaze into his eyes. "I don't regret making love with you. I want you to know that."

His heart did an extra double-tap. Thank God. "Neither do I."

"But there's so much going on at the moment, I'm finding it hard to process it all. Do you understand?"

Of course, he understood. If only he could stop that tiny part of him that yearned for something more. For something special. For someone who would truly accept him, warts and all. Penny might just be that person. His feelings for her were…complicated, but growing stronger every second they were together. He understood that whatever delicate thing was growing between them, it couldn't be forced, or it might break.

It was too hard to put his feelings into words, so he said, "Yeah. Let's eat dinner. We've got plenty of time to talk about this later." He planted one more kiss on those delectable lips, got up and ambled over to the kitchen to stir his spaghetti.

The pasta would be cooked soon, then he could stir in the sauce. Taking the vegetable scraps, he unlocked the door, meaning to throw them off the porch. The forest critters would enjoy the little tasty morsels.

Full dark had come to the forest; the light from the candles inside not penetrating far outside the door. A three-quarter moon rose over St Marys Peak. He took a moment to appreciate how the forest was transformed, bathed in the soft glow of moonlight.

A twig snapped somewhere outside the cabin perimeter,

and a night owl hooted, taking flight suddenly, its wings flapping noisily in the night.

His blood ran cold.

Stepping inside, he locked the door and thanked God for his decision not to start the generator. If that'd been turned on, he'd never have heard the noise.

Without explanation, he strode over to the sofa and picked Penny up.

"What are you doing?" she squeaked in alarm.

"There's someone outside. We need to hide." He headed for the bathroom. Not much protection, but at least it was one more door between them, and whoever was out there.

CHAPTER THIRTEEN

Penny felt completely helpless as Clayton set her down on the edge of the bath. What was going on? Two seconds ago, she'd been happily sitting on the sofa watching Clayton in an enlightening scene of domesticity, as he cooked them spaghetti. She could get used to that. Clayton cooking for her. Clayton looking after her. Clayton making love to her. The two of them in this intimate little cabin.

It was dark in here, both the candles still out in the main room. A small window above the sink let in a wash of moonlight. It was enough to make out shapes, but not details. Standing, she tested her ankle and let out a small cry of pain. It wouldn't hold her weight, so she sat back down, still processing Clayton's words.

"What do you mean? Who's out there?"

"I don't know." His eyes flicked around the room as he spoke. "But whoever it is, I don't think they're friendly." He opened the small cupboard door below the sink. What was he doing?

Then it struck her that perhaps he was looking for a weapon. Holy cow, should she be looking for a weapon, too? Her gaze landed on the small sink. Nothing there. The toilet. Could they rip the lid off and use that? The shower rail above her. It was a metal rod. That might work.

Penny had been listening intently for any sound or sign there really was someone outside. Clayton couldn't have imagined it, could he? How could anyone possibly have found them? Jude was the only one who knew where they were.

Gunfire erupted, the sound coming from the front of the cabin. Six or seven shots in rapid succession. Penny screamed.

"Get down." Clayton dragged her to the floor, covering her with his body.

There was silence for a few seconds, as if the man outside was listening and waiting for a reaction.

Another spray of gunfire sounded from outside. This time, two of the bullets pinged through the wall above them, and she screamed again, the sound muffled by the rug on the floor pressing into her face.

What were they going to do? They were trapped. With no way out. This man—or men, it sounded like there might be more than one of them, possibly the same two men from this morning—were going to storm into the cabin and murder them as they cowered on the floor of this tiny bathroom. There was more silence as the gunmen again waited to see if their shooting would draw them out. Watching to see if there was any movement. Perhaps they hoped they'd killed them.

Clayton was breathing heavily, crushing her with his weight. He was muttering something under his breath, but she was too terrified to concentrate on what he was saying. She wasn't sure what was worse; the silence or the ear-splitting bang of bullets slamming through the surrounding walls.

The rug beneath her cheek smelled musty and dust got up her nose, threatening to make her sneeze. She breathed in and out, feeling only the floor below her and Clayton's body above.

Clayton's body.

The floor.

Jude's words from earlier today came back in a torrent.

"Clayton, the floor." She struggled to move, but his massive body held her pinned in place.

"Stay still. I'll protect you," he whispered hoarsely.

She struggled harder, kicking out with her good leg. "Let me up. Clayton, the floor."

"What?" He moved slightly, just enough that she could lift her head and stare at him.

"There's a hatch. Jude said there was a hatch in here somewhere."

His eyes lit up with sudden comprehension. "You're a genius." Rolling to one side, he tugged at the round bathmat covering most of the floor. Penny shuffled backward, so he could remove the rug completely. And there it was. A square hatch cut into the wood, with a little brass ring bolted into a plank to pull it up.

"If you come out now, we'll spare the girl's life." A loud voice startled Penny. What were they doing? Trying to bargain with Clayton? There was no way she was letting him sacrifice himself for her.

But when she glanced over, he had his head down the hatch, looking at whatever was down there.

He came back up to his knees. "I think we can get out this way, by crawling underneath the floorboards." He stilled for a second, glancing between the door and the hatch. "Wait here, I'll be back in a second."

"What? Where are you…?" But it was too late, he'd already slipped through the door, closing it behind him, leaving her alone.

Then she heard Clayton say, "Stop shooting. If you promise not to hurt Penny, we'll come out."

"Clayton." she screamed. "No." What was he doing? Surely, he wasn't giving them both up to the hooligans outside. They'd murder them in cold blood. "Don't do this," she yelled. She stood and edged her way around the open hatch, using the wall as a support for her sprained ankle.

The man on the other side of the front door said something she didn't catch. She couldn't let Clayton do this. There was no way he she was allowing him to surrender himself to save her. She was just reaching for the door when it flew open and Clayton barged in.

"Oh, thank G—"

"What are you doing? Get in the hatch. Now." He grabbed her by the shoulders and forced her to sit down in the open square.

"Shit." She swung her legs down, using her hands to hold most of her weight. If she dropped through onto her sore ankle, it'd buckle beneath her. Quick. She had to do this quickly, so Clayton could come down, too. Whatever he'd been up to out there, she realized he was actually buying them more time.

The water heater was directly below her; probably situated so someone would only have to lean down through the hatch to be able to play with the switches on the side. She contorted her body around it, squeezing between the floorboards and the heater. It was dark down here. Really, really dark. Especially after Clayton closed the hatch. She couldn't see her hand in front of her face. Bare earth greeted her as she crawled around the metal water heater. Her face landed in a spiderweb and she gave a muffled scream, then began clawing at her face. She *hated* spiders. But she feared the men outside and their guns more. And fear was a great motivator. Taking a deep breath, she pressed on, leaving room for Clayton to drop down beside her. A row of boxes blocked her way. Jude had said Sam used this area for storage, as well.

Hopefully, they weren't completely hemmed in.

She felt his body collide with hers, then one of his hands felt along her back coming to rest on her shoulder.

"What now?" she whispered.

"The little shed at the back. I got the key. Jude said there were hunting knives in there."

Penny was all turned around. The little shed was at the back of the cabin, but she had no idea which direction to crawl in the dark. There wasn't a lot of room down here. She'd heard the term crawl space used for the area underneath the house, and now she understood why. On her hands and knees already, if she lifted her head, it banged against the floorboards above. Her hands dug into the dry earth below and she suppressed a shudder, not daring to think about what kind of things were crawling around down here. Penny thanked the forethought of the man who owned this cabin for building it on raised foundations. At least going in this direction, there were no more boxes to block their way.

A man's voice shouted something unintelligible. They were running out of time. The men outside were clearly becoming impatient.

"Let me past, I'll go first," Clayton whispered.

She was being brave about the spiderwebs, but if he wanted to go first and clear the way, then she would not argue. Clayton shuffled along in front of her and she reached out a hand to touch his shoe, reassuring herself he was close by. At least this was one thing she could do. Crawling meant she didn't have to put weight on her ankle. What she was going to do when they finally got out of here and she had to run for it, was another matter. Jude's words came back to haunt her. He'd been right, after all.

More gunfire erupted as the men finally worked out Penny and Clayton weren't going to give themselves up. Instinctively, she ducked her head. But at least the bullets were bouncing harmlessly around in the cabin above. They were safe for a little while.

A loud bang reverberated through the floorboards, like someone was trying to kick the door in. Quick, they needed to go faster. It wouldn't take long before their escape route was discovered.

A sliver of grayish light caught her eye. If that was moonlight, it meant they must be nearing the edge of the building. Emboldened by the idea of getting out from under the cabin, she crawled faster and promptly ran into Clayton's backside. Why had he stopped? The shed was just there, she could make out the square corner blocking the view to the right.

Loud footsteps sounded above their heads. Someone was inside. She pushed against Clayton, wanting him to move forward so they could get out before they were discovered.

Suddenly something moved, blocking the moonlight for a second, before proceeding on. A pair of legs. Someone was standing directly in their path of escape.

Shit. What now? One man was above them inside the cabin, while the other patrolled the perimeter of the building.

"Here's the key." Clayton turned around and fumbled for her palm in the dark. He pressed a cold, metal object into it. "I'm going to tackle him, take him down. And while I've got him occupied, I want you to unlock the shed and get inside. Arm yourself with whatever you can find," he whispered.

Penny shook her head. "I can't," she muttered. "My ankle." The idea was ridiculous. That man out there was armed with a gun. Clayton wouldn't stand a chance. "What happens if you—"

He stopped the rest of her words, his mouth over her hers, kissing her.

"I'd rather do this, than die like dogs down here. This way, you'll have a chance. Jude said the shed was full of hunting gear. He mentioned a bow and arrow, and there may even be a shotgun."

He was doing this to save her. She could tell by the tone of his voice. "Besides, if I can wrestle the gun away from him, we might have a chance."

If only she hadn't been so stupid. If her ankle were up to it, they could both try to escape into the forest. They'd stand a better chance running and hiding in dark places. But because of her, Clayton was forced to stand and fight.

She found his lips, funneling everything she couldn't say into that kiss. How much she admired him for what he was about to do. How much she wanted to yell at everyone on the ranch and in town because of how badly they'd misjudged him. He made one mistake and would pay for it for the rest of his life. If they ever got out of this, she was going to make sure people knew how strong and courageous he'd been today.

"I'm ready," she said, crawling closer to the edge.

Suddenly, headlights lit up the cabin. A car was coming down the gravel driveway. The owner of the legs shouted something and took off, running around to the front of the building. Who was it? No one knew they were here.

Clayton wasn't waiting to find out, however. He took the distraction offered and crawled out from under the cabin.

"Quick," he hissed, holding out his hand. She banged her head on the edge of a large wooden joist in her hurry to do as he said. Handing him the key, she hung onto the wooden logs of the rear wall of the cabin, steadying herself, getting ready to hobble after him.

The sound of gunshots reached them. The thugs must be firing at whoever was in the car. But then, wonder of wonders, there were panicked shouts as whoever it was returned fire. A gun battle was taking place at the front of the cabin. The loud retorts drowned out any sound Clayton was making, as he rattled the key in the padlock, eventually flinging the door open.

"Shit, I can't see a thing. It's too dark in here." She could hear him stumbling around in the small shed. "Shit, where's the fucking hunting knife?"

Pulling her phone out of her pocket, she crossed her fingers and turned it on. The *ding* as it came to life was the sweetest sound she'd ever heard. She hopped over to the door and clicked on the flashlight app, pointing it inside.

"Use this."

"You're a genius. That's twice in one day." If the circumstances were different, she would've smiled, perhaps even kissed him.

"Hurry," was all she said in reply. The sound of bullets whizzing through the air was deafening. They were still in mortal danger.

"I found the bow and arrow."

"Have you ever fired one before?" Penny asked.

"Only at the archery field at Stargazers. But I'm a pretty good shot."

Penny nearly laughed. On the ranch, they ran all kinds of activities for kids and adults alike. Archery was one of them. She'd tried it a few times, but most of her arrows went wide. Did he really think he could use that to stop these villains?

"I want you to stay here. Call 9-1-1 and stay hidden." He grabbed a slim bag of arrows and slung it over his shoulder, taking one and nocking it into the bow. Then he turned off the flashlight and handed her back her cell. "Promise me you'll stay here."

Penny crossed fingers behind her back. "Okay." Not on your life. She hadn't actually said the word *promise*. Did that count? She didn't think she could sit here and wait for whatever was coming next.

"Good. Because I don't know what I'd do if you got hurt.

You're…important to me, Penny."

Her heart constricted in her chest. But then he was gone, sliding away in the shadows, heading straight into danger. She was scared. Terrified. But as she sat there, contemplating her own mortality, it struck her. She'd spent the past two years being apprehensive and alone. No, it was longer than that. For most of the four years before that, she'd also lived in trepidation, waiting for Mitch's next controlling deed. And look where that had gotten her. Clayton was out there who was prepared to put it all on the line for her. He must be scared, too. The difference was, he didn't let that fear control him or define him.

She didn't want to live in fear anymore. She wanted to be in control of her own destiny. Plus, she had skills she shouldn't let go to waste.

Damned if she was going to let Clayton do this alone. Right before he turned off the flashlight, she noticed a set of hunting knives laid out on a small bench inside the shed. Using the door frame as a support, she felt around until her fingers touched the closest one. Unsheathing it, she gripped the hilt in her right hand. Hefting it up and down a few times, she tested the weight. Yep, definitely heavy enough to throw with a large enough blade to do damage. Holding on to the cabin wall as she hobbled around the corner of the building. She dialed 9-1-1, and put the cell to her ear, even as she kept moving. She would do as Clayton asked and get the cops here as soon as she could, but she also had another priority.

She understood this puny knife would be no match for the thugs' guns. And her unsteady, hobbling gait meant there was no way she was getting away quickly if it were required. But she went anyway, because to stay behind and cower in the shed while her man was out there getting shot at was unthinkable.

CHAPTER FOURTEEN

Clayton crouched by the corner of the front porch. This was like nothing else he'd ever experienced. He was in the middle of an actual, real-life, gun fight. It was extremely loud, gunshots ringing in his ears, men shouting hoarsely, and his bowels shivered every time he heard a bullet whiz through the air nearby. Darkness hampered his ability to assess the situation. The three-quarter moon threw down its silvery light, but it made everything shadowy and illusory. He couldn't see any of the shooters. And he couldn't very well shoot anyone with an arrow if he couldn't see them.

So, he concentrated on where the bullets were coming from. How many men were out there? If it was Dmytro's men, then hopefully it was only the two they'd seen earlier this morning. When they'd been in the crawl space below the cabin, they'd heard one man stomping around upstairs and then seen the other guarding the rear of the cabin. Which made two. Unless they'd brought additional backup and they were hiding somewhere out in the forest. Clayton was counting on only two.

The car that'd distracted the killers was parked at an angle across the dirt driveway, with headlights turned off, probably to make the driver less of a target. Clayton was stunned to see that it was the police cruiser.

Jude had come back.

For what reason, Clayton had no idea, but he wanted to kiss the man right now. God, he hoped he'd radioed for backup. Because they needed all the help they could get. Jude was keeping both of Dmytro's thugs pinned down, returning their gunfire while yelling that he was a state police officer and demanding they lay down their weapons and surrender. Clayton liked his friend's optimism. He guessed it was something to do with protocol, declaring who he was and what he wanted.

A shadow reared up behind the trunk of the cruiser—Clayton assumed it was Jude's head—and four bullets were fired in quick succession toward a substantial, old pine tree to the right of the cabin, about fifty yards away. Someone behind the tree returned fire, and Jude ducked his head back down.

Another set of gunfire came from the other side of the clearing. The second shooter was taking cover behind a limestone outcrop that reared twelve or more feet into the air. There weren't a lot of places to hide; this cabin was small, so the men had taken themselves into the forest. Jude swung around and loosed a few bullets in his direction. Jude was on his own; it'd take a lot of skill to keep both these men at bay at once.

Clayton focused on the shadow behind the large tree. It moved, dashing to another tree, slightly higher up the slope. Now he was sixty yards away. It was around the same distance the archery targets had been at the outdoor range at Stargazers. The shooter behind the rocks sent out another volley and Jude returned fire. Clayton narrowed his eyes, the guy on his right was working his way deeper into the forest. But why?

Then it dawned on him. The thug was sneaking around

behind Jude, perhaps hoping to take him by surprise. And even if Jude figured it out, it'd be almost impossible for him to hold off two men firing at him from completely opposite directions.

He couldn't let this thug get behind Jude. Clayton could see the man clearly now, sheltering behind the trunk of a pine tree. He was hiding from Jude, but didn't realize Clayton could see him because the angles were different. It was now or never. The man was as clear as he was ever going to be.

Clayton stood and took a few steps into the open. He knew he was making himself an open target, but he couldn't fire the bow any other way. Lifting it to his shoulder, he drew back the bowstring and held his breath, then let the arrow fly. There was a wooden *thunk* and the man standing by the tree flinched and ducked, swearing loudly.

Shit, he'd hit the tree.

Clayton already had another arrow nocked and took aim again.

The dark shadow of the man by the tree turned to face Clayton, gun raised, pointed directly at him.

"Hey, over here." Penny stepped out from behind the front porch and the man with the gun looked her way. It was the split-second Clayton needed.

He narrowed his focus and loosed the arrow. There was a scream of agony. The man fell in a heap on the ground, groaning.

He swung around. "Penny, get down," he yelled. She was going to get herself killed. It was stupid. And amazingly courageous. She must have taken cover underneath the raised front porch. It wasn't high off the ground, so she could've crawled under there.

Shots rang out around his head, and belatedly he fell to his knees and scrambled back to the relative safety of the corner of the cabin. In those few seconds of elation—he'd actually managed to hit the guy with his arrow—he'd forgotten all about the second thug.

Was the other guy dead? Or at the very least, incapacitated? He had no clue what to do next. Should he check on the man by the tree? Disarm him, so he couldn't keep shooting? Or should he concentrate on the other man behind the rocks? But first, he needed to convince Penny to stay out of sight. He couldn't leave her so totally unprotected, and he couldn't have her putting herself in danger like that again. Did he dare cut across the front of the cabin to get to her? That guy behind the rocks was most likely still aiming for him.

"Clayton, is that you?" Jude yelled.

"Yeah," Clayton shouted back, his gaze flicking between the spot where he'd felled the man with the arrow and the rocky outcrop. The man had stopped moaning. Clayton had no idea if that was good or bad.

"What sort of weapon are you using?"

Clayton thought about that for a second. If he told Jude, then the other thug would also know. Would that put him at a disadvantage?

"Bow and arrow," he finally replied.

There was a second of surprised hesitation. "Great. Keep it trained on the bastard behind the rocks, I'm coming to you. Backup is on the way, they'll be here any minute."

What? Clayton's guts clenched in a moment of panic. Why would Jude put himself in danger like that? He should stay where he was, behind the safety of his vehicle. But then, he reminded himself, he'd already shot one guy. He could do this. He just needed to stay calm. He was in no position to argue. The thought of reinforcements buoyed him, but he knew Jude was probably exaggerating, they were at least forty-five minutes from town. It'd be a while yet before anyone got here.

Before Clayton had more than a second to compose himself —and before he could yell out to Penny to stay where she was—Jude had stood and come around to the front of his cruiser, firing at the large heap of boulders. Clayton stood and nocked an arrow, pointing it in the same direction, although he couldn't get a clear line on the guy behind the rocks. All he could really see was two shadowy arms and part of a shoulder as the thug shot at Jude.

Shit. Clayton took aim and let the arrow go. It glanced off the rock near the man's shoulder, but it was enough to send him ducking for cover.

Jude ran around the edge of the clearing, using the scattered trees as minimal cover, ducking and weaving, sending off a shot when he could. Clayton tore his gaze away from the deputy and sent off another arrow. This one also ricocheted off the rocks and flew at an angle into the forest, hopefully keeping the thug pinned behind his shelter.

Tearing his eyes away from the limestone for a second, Clayton watched Jude's progress. He was more than half-way to them; he was going to make it.

Three gunshots echoed around the clearing, and Jude went down. He lay writhing on the dirt, crying out in pain.

Fuck. By the time Clayton looked back to where the thug was hiding, he'd hunkered down out of sight. In the two seconds Clayton had taken his eyes off him, the thug had pounced. Now Jude was lying out in the open, injured and completely at the other man's mercy.

There was nothing else for it. Clayton stepped away from the cover of the building and walked steadily toward the rocks. If that man showed even an eyebrow, he was going to take him out. He hoped.

Suddenly, there was a shout, and the thug stumbled forward, away from the cover of the boulders. Right into Clayton's line of sight.

He let go the arrow. The shot was off target, too low, and it lodged in the man's thigh, instead of his chest, where he'd been aiming. But it did the job, and the man fell back with a cry, clutching at his leg with one hand and at his shoulder with the other.

But why had he stumbled forward?

Nocking another arrow, he slowly advanced toward the man on the ground. He had an arrow sticking out of his leg and what looked to be a knife sticking out of his back, on the right of his shoulder blade.

The reason the man had stumbled directly into Clayton's line of sight appeared around the edge of the rocks.

Penny.

"What the…?" Clayton was lost for words.

"I told you I was good at throwing knives," she said.

"I surrender," the man yelled. "Get me a fucking ambulance, will you?"

The man's gun was lying in the dirt where he'd dropped it when the arrow hit him. Clayton went over and picked it up, leaning the bow and arrows up against the boulders. This would be a much better weapon. He pointed it at the man on the ground.

"You stay right there."

"I'm not going fucking anywhere. I've got an arrow in my fucking leg," the guy bellowed.

Clayton went over and put an arm around Penny's shoulder, helping her hobble to where Jude lay on the ground closer to the cabin. He kept one eye on the dude on the ground until he lowered Penny down next to Jude.

"Can you help him?" he asked. "I'll call an ambulance and go and check on the other guy behind the tree."

"Of course." Penny was already on her hands and knees, leaning over Jude. "Where are you shot?" she asked, voice full of professional purpose. "We have to stop the bleeding."

"In the leg, my calf." Jude spoke with a grimace, clearly in a lot of pain. "Clayton," the deputy called as he spun away. "Use the radio in my cruiser. Update everyone and tell them we'll need at least two ambulances."

"I already called them. They're on their way." Penny looked up momentarily before getting back to work on Jude's leg.

"Call them again," Jude said. "Bring the sheriff's office up to speed."

"Will do. What about the guy over there? Should I tie him up?" Clayton had no idea what to do with this whole mess.

"No, I'll keep an eye on him," Jude raised his gun, which he still held in his right hand. "If he moves, I'll shoot him," he said in a voice loud enough for the thug to hear. They heard a groan by way of reply.

Clayton made his way toward the cruiser but stopped at the big tree half-way around the clearing on the way. He approached slowly and carefully, gun at the ready. A dark, unmoving lump lay at the base of the tree trunk. He prodded it with his toe. Nothing. He prodded again, harder this time. Still nothing.

Gun in one hand pointed at the lump, he leaned in and slowly rolled the man over. An arrow stuck straight out of his chest. Jesus. He'd shot him in the heart. There was no sign of life. Had he killed him?

"The ambulance is on its way," Clayton confirmed, returning from the cruiser a few minutes later, after first checking on the guy Penny had knifed. He was still lying on the ground, moaning. There was no way he was going to attempt an escape. "Deputy Nomad and your trainee, Scott, will be here in around five minutes."

"Thank you," Jude ground out between gritted teeth. Penny had a rag of some kind pressed over Jude's leg as she knelt beside him. It took Clayton a second to realize she'd torn a strip off the bottom of her T-shirt, because he could see a wide band of pale skin exposed in the moonlight.

"And thank you," Penny said. "Thank you for coming back. How did you know we needed help?"

"I didn't. I turned around because I got some news over the radio and I was coming back to tell you. When I saw a sedan parked farther up the forest road, I had a feeling you might be in trouble. They must've stolen another car and then walked the rest of the way in so as not to alert you. I knew they couldn't have been here too long, otherwise I would've passed them on the road. They must've followed me and waited out on the highway until I came back out. I'm so sorry, guys."

"What was so important you had to come right back and tell us?" Clayton asked.

Jude hesitated for a heartbeat. "I was coming back to tell you Dmytro is dead."

"What?" Clayton whipped his head around from where he'd been watching the other thug struggle weakly into a sitting position.

"There was a riot up at the prison tonight. Dmytro was killed in the mêlée. The warden up at Missoula thinks it might've been an intentional hit. Someone started the riot, so one of Dmytro's competitors could have a shot at him. These mob bosses are always trying to do each other in."

Clayton couldn't believe it. His knees suddenly felt weak, and he wanted to sit. Was it possible all his troubles could completely vanish, just like that? With Dmytro gone, there would be no trial, and he no longer had to fear the mob boss would send more thugs after him.

"These guys obviously didn't get the memo that their boss was dead. They'll be pretty pissed when they find out they did this all for nothing." Jude grimaced and Clayton wondered if it was from the pain or from the useless waste of life.

"That's great. Isn't it?" Penny looked up from where she was keeping the pressure on Jude's leg.

"Yes." Clayton nodded slowly. "It means he's off my tail." It meant his life could go back to normal. Whatever normal looked like, now. He tipped his head back to stare at the moon. Normality. That would be nice.

The guy with the arrow in his leg groaned and called out, "How long until that fucking ambulance gets here?"

Clayton ignored him, but it spiked an interesting question in his mind. "How did you get over there with your sore ankle?" Clayton asked, pointing at the pile of boulders. He'd been intrigued ever since she'd appeared out of the shadows behind the rock. He certainly hadn't seen her leave the safety of the cabin.

"I crawled." She shrugged. "It was the easiest way with my ankle, and it kept me out of sight. I stayed behind those small bushes over there, and then crept through the long grass until I reached the boulders. You guys were all so caught up in your shooting match, no one had time to notice me. Which was exactly what I wanted."

"Jesus," Jude said, a hint of awe in his tone. "You've got yourself one special lady there. I wouldn't be letting her go in a hurry."

Penny looked up at Clayton, biting her lip, but said nothing.

Clayton was startled by Jude's words. Not because the deputy recognized Penny was an exceptional woman; Clayton already knew that. He was startled by the way Jude had called her *his lady*. Was she his? He had no idea. The words sent a pulse of hot longing through him, and he suddenly knew without a doubt he wanted her to be his. Did she want the same thing?

CHAPTER FIFTEEN

Penny yawned and rolled over. Her body wanted to keep sleeping, but her mind had other ideas. Cracking one eye open, she glared at the sunshine streaming in through a slit in the curtains. She checked her phone to see that it was nearly ten a.m.

Groaning, she sat up in bed, careful of her sore ankle—which was now securely strapped—fluffing the pillows up behind her back so she could lean against the wall. Casting her gaze around the familiar room she shared with Stella, she pulled the blankets up a little more snugly around her. It was so wonderful to be back on the ranch. Stella's bed was neatly made, she must've been as quiet as a mouse this morning when she got up for her shift in the kitchen. Penny hadn't heard a thing.

It was Friday morning. Naomi had given her the next few days off to recover. But Penny had too much to do before the wedding tomorrow to take Naomi's threat of tying her to the bed if she didn't rest seriously.

It seemed hard to believe it'd only been forty-eight hours since Mitch had tried to kidnap her. So much had happened in those two days. She'd spent most of yesterday and the night before either in the hospital, or being interviewed by the sheriff, other detectives from Missoula, FBI agents, and it seemed anyone else who was even remotely involved with this case.

After the ambulances had come and taken Jude and the men who'd been trying to kill them away, she and Clayton had also been taken to the hospital to be checked out. A nice young doctor had confirmed her ankle was only sprained, which was a relief. He told her to stay off it as much as possible over the next few days and weeks. She'd smiled at him and tried not to roll her eyes. He obviously had no idea what it meant to be a bridesmaid.

Clayton had come in after the doctor left and told her that Jude was going to be fine. He was in surgery, and the doctors had warned he'd need a few months of rehab and recovery, but he could go back to working as a deputy soon. Clayton had little information about the man she'd knifed in the back, apart from the fact he was going to live. Police and FBI agents had swarmed through the hospital all night long, and after the doctor had declared she was fine to leave, she and Clayton had been taken back to the sheriff's office to be debriefed. Penny had talked until her voice was almost gone, reliving the past few hours over and over again. They were allowed to catch a few hours' sleep in Jude's office; Penny curled up on the floor with Jude's coat under her head, and Clayton slumped in Jude's chair. Then they'd been taken back to the cabin in the woods once it was light, to go over the whole scenario time after time, until Penny's head hurt.

All she really wanted to do was to block the whole, terrifying night from her memory. That night had been... There were no words to explain the confusing, violent whirlwind that'd swept her up and away.

She wanted to talk to Clayton. He, alone, might understand how she was feeling. Clayton had been her rock yesterday, hovering nearby like a mother hen, refusing to leave her side, and yelling at one young police officer when he demanded that Penny show him exactly how she'd crawled to the limestone outcrop with the knife in her hand.

Her cell sat on her bedside table, and she contemplated calling him. Clayton had said she could, no matter what time it was, no matter what the problem. If she ever wanted to talk, then he was there for her.

And she wanted to talk to him. Wanted to see him, hear his voice, hold him.

What was going to happen to them now? Were their lives going back to normal? If she stayed at Stargazers—and that was still a big if—would she see him again? Or would they both pretend this whole thing never happened?

Her twenty-four hours spent with him had been a revelation. The one thing that'd become crystal-clear was that she wanted more of Clayton. But she had no idea what a picture of her life with him in it was supposed to look like.

To hell with it. She picked up her cell. The phone rang for so long she nearly hung up.

"Hello," said a groggy voice. Holy cow, he must've been asleep. Just because her frantic mind was going overtime, she shouldn't have assumed his would be, too.

"I'm so sorry, Clayton, did I wake you?"

"Penny, hi." The grogginess seemed to clear quickly as he heard her voice. "I was going to get up soon, anyway. Don't worry about it. How are you?"

"I'm not sure," she said ruefully. There was no point in hiding how she felt from Clayton, he would understand. "I guess I'm feeling a little lost. And overwhelmed. And really confused." She didn't want to add that the confusion was mainly caused by her feelings for him.

"I know what you mean."

Penny could almost picture Clayton sitting up in bed. She'd glimpsed his bedroom on her way to use the bathroom the other day—she'd known it was his and not his roommate Harry's because she'd seen a pair of his worn cowboy boots resting at the foot of his bed. His hair would be ruffled from sleep. And she could picture his glorious naked chest as he lay back against the pillows, that sprinkling of curls covering muscular pecs and those washboard abs flexing slightly as he sat up. Mmm.

"Penny, are you still there?"

Oh, damn, she'd been caught daydreaming and missed his previous words. God, she wanted to see him right now, so badly it hurt.

"Yes, yes, sorry." Penny had a sudden thought, so clear, it was like a bell going off in her head. Of course, why hadn't she thought of this earlier. "Clayton, are you free this Saturday afternoon?"

"Ah, yes, why?" She could hear by his tone he had no idea where she was going with this.

A bubble of excitement swelled in her chest. This was the right thing to do.

"I was wondering if you would be my date for the wedding?"

There was a heartbeat of silence. Then another. She crossed her fingers and hoped he wasn't going to turn her down.

"You mean at Cat and Levi's wedding?"

"Yes. I need a date, and I want it to be you."

"Is Cat okay with this?"

"Of course, she is," Penny lied. She wasn't even going to ask Cat's permission on this one. It might be Cat and Levi's day, but it was also a little bit hers, and it was time this subtle innuendo and suspicion surrounding Clayton ended. They needed to stop tarring Clayton with the same brush as Alex and his brother Cyrus. Clayton hadn't lit any of those fires. It wasn't his fault that Alex had framed him. Clayton had only ever had the ranch's best interests at heart. He loved this ranch; it was so unfair that it'd all been taken away from him. Penny was going to try to remedy that.

"Are you sure? Because I don't want Levi punching me out when he sees I've crashed his wedding."

"If he does, he'll have me to answer to." Penny was appalled that Clayton thought Levi would do that. Perhaps Clayton had reason to be misguided when it came to Levi, he'd never gotten to know him, after all. Levi was a fair and generous man, who thought things through with deep introspection. He held no grudge against Clayton, she knew because she'd asked him one day. Unlike Cat. Cat was still dark at Clayton because he'd tried to abduct her. She couldn't see past his rash act to the desperation that'd impaired his normally good judgement. But Penny could talk Cat around, she knew she could. "Don't worry, I've got it all sorted." She was lying again, but she was so hungry to see Clayton, she knew she could work this out.

"Um… Okay, if you're sure." She could hear his hesitancy. And it wasn't only to do with Cat and Levi. She knew Clayton was worried how he'd be received by everyone at Stargazer, especially Dean and Naomi. During their short time at the cabin, he'd confided in her just how sorry he was that he'd lost Dean's trust. How much he'd like to regain it one day. Well, she was going to help him do that.

"I think it will be good, Clayton. For everyone." She hoped she'd conveyed to him she had his back, and that this might even be a way to turn how people at Stargazer viewed him around. He didn't say anything more, but his doubt was telegraphed by his silence on the other end of the phone.

"What about Mitch? Are you still worried about him?" Clayton changed the subject.

Penny sat up a little straighter in bed. She'd had a long discussion with Deputy Susan Nomad about Mitch yesterday afternoon, after all the debriefings about the shooting. Susan had said there'd been no sign of her ex over the past twenty-four hours, but they still couldn't rule him out as a potential threat. Penny was no longer scared of Mitch. After what she'd lived through in the past few days, Mitch was small potatoes.

"I think I'll be safe enough, as long as I stay on the ranch. Mitch is a bully and a psycho, but he won't dare show his face here again, not with the hordes of people about to descend for the wedding. I'll be safe enough for now. I'll think about what to do about him after."

"Are you sure?"

"Yes, I'm sure." She'd decided to stop being afraid. If the previous night had taught her anything, it was that she was stronger than she thought. If she could handle a dangerous thug armed with a gun, then she could handle Mitch with no problem. He'd had a hold over her, but it'd been her mind holding her hostage to his threats. And Clayton had showed her there were good men out there, who didn't need to belittle or manipulate a woman to feed their dominant male ego.

Besides all that, Penny no longer had a car after Mitch had torched hers. Even if she wanted to leave, she would have to arrange some other form of transportation. Naomi had said she would help her fill out the insurance paperwork, so she could at least afford to buy a new car. But that would take time. Without a car, she was pretty much stuck here, for a while at least.

They talked for nearly half an hour, about how Clayton had been given the next few days off work, the same as her, and how Harry hadn't believed him at first when he'd come home with his fantastic tale of hitmen and shootouts. She talked about her growing list of things she needed to do before the wedding. It was so lovely to hear his voice; she kept asking questions long after the important ones ran out, to keep him on the phone a bit longer.

At the sound of footsteps in the hallway, Penny finally accepted it was time to end the call and told Clayton she had to go. She said goodbye just as Stella poked her head around the door.

"Oh, good, you're awake." Stella came all the way into the bedroom carrying a tray. "I brought you some breakfast, courtesy of Joseph. And me, of course."

Stella was so sweet; she could see the concern etched around the other woman's eyes. They'd all been so worried about Penny when she called to give her an abbreviated version of Mitch's near abduction the other day. Then, when she also told them she was with Clayton, Stella admitted that she'd been especially terrified. Penny decided that after what she'd been through with Wyatt, she had every right to be.

Penny's stomach rumbled loudly. She'd hardly eaten at all in the past two days. Stella lay the tray on Penny's lap and then sat on her own bed while Penny ate. Oh, sweet baby Jesus, there was a freshly cooked omelette—Stella made the best omelettes on the planet—hot toast, slathered with butter, and the best part of all, a large mug of brewed coffee with lots of cream and sugar, just the way she liked it.

"Dean and Naomi would like to talk to you, when you're ready." Stella smiled as she watched Penny devour her breakfast.

"Good, because I want to talk to them, too," Penny said through a mouthful of food.

Half an hour later, Penny had showered and dressed and found out the hard way that crutches weren't as easy to use as they looked, as she crossed the gravel driveway between the staff quarters and the lodge.

By the time she'd negotiated a path through the kitchen—answering Joseph and Violet's questions on her way—and then down the hallway and across the grand foyer to knock on the door to Dean's office, she was getting the hang of them.

"Hi, Penny." Naomi greeted her with a warm hug. "So good to see you up and around again." The older woman tried to hide it, but Penny noticed her concerned glance down at her ankle.

"How are you feeling today?" Dean hovered, laying a hand on her shoulder, his genial face also etched with concern. "We were worried about you after you called Naomi to tell her about your ex-husband. And when we heard you were with Clayton… Well, let's just say our worry wasn't lessened any. But we never in a million years thought you'd be shot at by mobsters. You poor girl, here take my seat." Dean led her over to his leather chair, and against her protests, almost pushed her into it. That was so like Dean, he would give you the shirt off his back if he thought you needed it.

"I'm fine now, really," she replied. But something Dean had said annoyed her, and it needed to be addressed. Right away, before they got any more ideas that this had all been Clayton's fault. "I was scared, I admit that. But I need you to know that if Clayton hadn't been there, I'd be dead. He saved me. He saved both of us."

"Yes, but Clayton was also the reason you were in the predicament in the first place," Naomi said gently.

The irony wasn't lost on Penny.

"That's true." She nodded. "But I was only involved because he saved me from Mitch. Twice. The thugs forced his hand by threatening me. What I'm trying to say, is that Clayton did everything he could to protect me. He laid his life on the line for me. And for Jude. He's a good man, Dean. He doesn't deserve all this continued condemnation."

Dean tapped his lip with a finger and stared at Penny. "He worked hard when he was with us on the ranch, I was impressed by his knowledge and horsemanship. I never doubted his work ethic for a second."

"Or his character," Naomi interjected. "We all liked Clayton."

"Until you didn't," Penny said.

"Yes, until we thought he was the arsonist," Dean agreed. "I admit, I could never truly fathom why he would attack the ranch."

"I think you really need to give him another chance." Penny lay her cards on the table, she wasn't going to leave this alone. "He loves this ranch and it cuts deep that he lost your trust."

"I'll think about it," Dean promised.

Dean was a fair-minded man. Penny hoped he'd do as he said and really consider it. Clayton deserved their forgiveness.

"But we have more pressing things on our plate at the moment," Naomi said, smoothly changing the subject.

"Yes, the wedding." Penny turned to Naomi, her mind shifting gears into bridesmaid mode. Some of Cat and Levi's family and friends would arrive tonight, and things needed to be set in motion to make sure their stay at Stargazers was a great one. The ranch was closed to tourists over the coming weekend, so they could cater for the wedding.

"I know you told me to take it easy, but there's so much to be done. And you know I'm the best person to do it." Penny held up a hand as Naomi opened her mouth. "I won't take no for an answer. And before you say it, I'll be fine getting around on my crutches. A bit slower than usual, perhaps, but I can still do it all." Penny sat back, locking eyes with Naomi, hoping and praying she'd say yes.

Naomi gave a light laugh. "I knew you'd still want to be involved," she said, also leaning back in her chair. "So, I've arranged for Dale to be at your beck and call. He can be your legs for you, to save you having to run all over the ranch.

And if you need anything in town, he can pick it up."

"Oh, thank you." That was actually a great idea. Dale normally worked with the cattle and the horse-riding activities on the ranch. But with no paying guests around for the next few days, there was less for him to do. It was a perfect solution.

As if he could read Naomi's mind, there was a knock at the door and Dale came in, wearing his cowboy hat and boots. The guy was gorgeous, and with those dimples in his cheeks, and that Australian accent, Penny had seen many a woman go weak at the knees whenever he walked into the room. But after getting to know him over the past few years, she also knew that while he was cocky on the outside, it was only to cover the fact he was really a shy guy.

"Hi, Dale." She waved at him from her chair and he leaned back on the sideboard and gave her a cheeky grin in return.

Naomi gave him a motherly smile, standing and going over to pick a stray bit of hay from his shirt.

"We're going to miss our Dale," Naomi said wistfully.

"Oh?" Penny cocked her head in his direction.

"We haven't announced it to the rest of the staff yet, so keep this to yourself." Naomi frowned, as if she realized she'd slipped up.

"Of course," Penny agreed.

"Dale is going back to Australia. His mom, Dean's sister, needs him to help her run the station over there."

"Oh." Penny's mind was going a million miles an hour. "So, you'll be needing a new ranch hand, then?" She caught Dean's gaze, and he pursed his lips. "That's interesting."

CHAPTER SIXTEEN

Clayton shifted from one foot to the other, gravel crunching under his shiny, black shoes. He pulled at his collar and fanned himself with his Stetson. Why, oh why, had he agreed to come to this wedding? It was the first day of summer, and here he was, sweating in a black suit. Who in their right mind thought up this torturous piece of clothing? He'd be much more comfortable in jeans and a plaid shirt. He'd arrived at Stargazers twenty minutes ago, but hadn't dared to enter the lodge, and so instead elected to wait outside the back door for Penny.

Cat's motorcycle sat, black and gleaming on the gravel nearby. Clayton knew better than to touch it. It was Cat's baby; she'd know if he left a single fingerprint on it. Penny had told him that Cat was going to ride up the aisle on her motorcycle and Clayton had laughed. It was just so Cat.

Images of him and Cat a little over a year ago swam in front of his vision. He'd held a knife to her throat. He pressed his hands into his stomach when he thought of what he'd done. All logic and sanity had left him that night. The urge to clear his name had been so strong. He was innocent. How could they have not believed him? He'd really only wanted to talk to Cat, persuade her to get Levi to go to the sheriff and tell him the truth. Because he'd been so certain that Cat and Levi knew the truth. Levi must've seen whoever had attacked him that night, when his house was burned down and known it wasn't Clayton. He'd convinced himself that Cat and Levi had it in for him, were intentionally holding out so he was arrested. That they were part of the conspiracy trying to put him in jail. He hadn't had any clear plan when he'd intercepted Cat. If Levi hadn't turned up and they'd both overpowered him, Clayton wasn't sure what he would've done next. Perhaps he would've seen sense and walked away, who knew? It was the darkest moment of his life. And the worst part was that it still defined the way he lived today.

He was determined to ask Cat's forgiveness today. After the ceremony, during the reception, he would go up to her. Face his wrongs. Apologize unreservedly. It was all he could do. All he had left. If she turned him down, so be it. But he had to at least try.

A buzz of conversation could be heard lower down in the garden. Wedding guests were congregating in the clearing. Now and then, he glimpsed a colorful dress through the trees. Not only was he hot and sweating, he was damn near terrified of coming face-to-face with the Stargazer staff. How would they receive him? Would they glower and turn their backs?

This was a stupid idea. He tugged at the bow tie again, using all his will not to pull the damn thing right off.

Then Penny emerged through the door and all his petty grievances disappeared. Her pale-green bridesmaid dress suited her perfectly. It floated around her knees and hugged her hips in exactly the right places. He could see her eyes clearly, now she was no longer wearing those glasses as part of her disguise. Her eyes were a summer blue, and she'd done something amazing with her hair. It was loose but fell in soft curls around her face. She looked stunning.

She'd refused to use the crutches today, but had finally conceded to a walking cane, which she was now waving around agitatedly in the air at Stella and Emily, who were following behind. He'd had to listen to her lamenting over the phone last night that she was also wearing flats today, instead of the gorgeous high heels she'd picked out. Clayton had reminded her that at least she was able to go to the wedding and Penny had stopped grumbling. He wouldn't dare say that her sprained ankle resulted from her own lapse of judgement. Because she'd been scared and confused back at the cabin; he'd done plenty of stupid things in his lifetime, and he wasn't even being hunted by a mob boss at the time.

When she saw Clayton waiting for her, she stopped and stared. There was a moment of awkward silence until Stella came around Penny and grinned at him.

"We'll see you down at the clearing," Stella said, tugging on Emily's hand to make sure she followed. "Tom and Wyatt are already there, helping to get the guests seated," Stella continued, but Penny didn't seem to be listening, she was still staring at Clayton. "And Dale is already down by the parking lot with Star, waiting for Levi, so he can ride him in." Clayton wasn't sure if this information was supposed to be for him, or Penny.

Levi had said that if Cat could ride her motorcycle into the ceremony, then he was going to gallop up on his white steed. The way Penny told it over the phone, she said that Cat had snorted in disgust and declared that the ranch didn't own a white horse, and she didn't need rescuing by some knight in shining armor, either. Clayton agreed with that wholeheartedly, Cat could definitely look after herself, but surely, she had to acknowledge the romance of his gesture.

"Thanks," Clayton replied, when Penny still said nothing. "We'll see you down there in a second."

It wasn't until Stella and Emily disappeared down the

path, tottering on their high heels and giggling like schoolgirls, that Penny finally spoke. "Wow." She stepped backward and let her eyes trace a lazy path from his toes right up to his head. "I thought you might look good in a suit. But, holy cow, you look even better than I imagined."

Suddenly, he didn't hate the outfit so much.

Her gaze devoured him, and on instinct he wrapped his arms around her waist. "You look pretty hot yourself," he whispered in her ear. "I've been dreaming about kissing you for the past two days. But I don't want to ruin your makeup." It was true, he hadn't been able to get her off his mind. He hadn't meant to tell her that, but she looked so gorgeous, how could he not?

"I've been thinking about kissing you, too," she breathed, standing on tiptoe and reaching for his mouth, letting her cane drop heedlessly to the ground. She tasted like spearmint, as if she'd just brushed her teeth, and pink lip gloss. A surge of craving heated his veins. Her body molded tight against his, and he held her suspended into his chest, taking most of her weight, mindful of her sore ankle.

The door opened suddenly behind them, and Clayton looked up to see Dean and Naomi walk out. Shit, they'd been caught red-handed. By the boss, no less. He let Penny go, bending down to retrieve her cane.

"Hello, Clayton, you look nice." Naomi showed not even a hint of surprise or animosity that he was here as she smiled brightly.

"Ah… Hi, Naomi, good to see you." He raised his hat and nodded at her. Penny said that everyone knew he was coming today, and they were all fine with it. But being told that over the phone and seeing it for himself were two different things.

Dean held out his hand, and Clayton shook it. "Glad you could be here today, Clayton. I hear we owe you a debt of gratitude for looking after Penny." Dean's grip was firm and warm. It heartened Clayton to think that perhaps there was forgiveness in that handshake.

"Penny was pretty good at looking after herself," Clayton replied. "But I am glad to be here, sir." It was as if a small part of the black cloud hovering over Clayton's life lifted in that moment. It *was* good to be here.

"We'll see you down there. Don't be too long, now." Dean and Naomi headed for the path, hand in hand. Had Dean just winked at him?

He returned his concentration to Penny, who had an odd smile on her face. "I'd better get you down to the ceremony, right now."

"Yes, Cat will be out any moment. The three bridesmaids are supposed to precede her down the aisle as she rides up on her motorcycle. So, I need to be at the edge of the clearing by then." Penny smiled brightly and extended her hand. He hooked it through his elbow and helped her down the pathway. It was probably a good idea if he was out of sight by the time Cat came out of the lodge. He briefly wondered if she would wear black leathers to her own wedding, or would she be riding in a white dress? No, even Cat wouldn't do that. Would she?

Penny seemed to be walking better today, so her ankle must be on the mend. These gardens were Naomi's pride and joy. She'd hired a landscape designer to help bring her dream to life, and it was now one of the best country gardens in the county. The path was laid with soft sawdust and coiled through tall Douglas-fir and western larch, planted with an understory of sagebrush and juniper. There was a small, burbling stream meandering through the shade, silver fish darting beneath the outcrops of rocks. At night, the garden lit up, with craftily hidden solar lights that showcased the huge buttress of a tree or hung in the branches like a swarm of fireflies. But the lifelike bronze statues were the highlight of the garden. A hare scampering up a grassy knoll. A doe and her fawn peeking out from a small clearing. An enormous grizzly bear raising a paw to the sky. Naomi had them commissioned from a local sculptor and they brought the place to life. Back when Clayton had worked on the ranch, he would often amble through these gardens in wonder.

They walked in companionable silence through the forest, a warm breeze tickling the branches. It was the perfect day for a wedding. Dean and Naomi's voices could be heard somewhere in front, as they strolled toward the clearing. The path took them in a loop, skimming the edge of the parking lot, and Clayton could see Dale holding Star, who was flicking his ears in agitation, a hundred yards away on the grassy verge in the corner of the lot. Levi stood nearby, looking down at his phone, perhaps waiting for the go-ahead to mount up and ride into the clearing. He didn't look nervous at all. Actually, he had a sappy grin on his face.

Penny raised a hand and waved at Dale, who waved back. Oh, to hell with it. Clayton gave a quick wave, as well. Dale flashed a welcoming grin in his direction. Dale had only arrived at Stargazers from Australia a few months before Clayton had gone on the run. Even though he hadn't got to know the guy particularly well, he'd liked him from the start. They'd gone into town on their days off to have a friendly drink at the local bar. And Dale was an amazing horseman. Clayton sometimes thought he might go to Australia to learn a few tips from their cowboys over there.

Levi looked up from his cell and stared. For a second, Clayton thought he might turn away. But he, too, raised his hand in greeting. Clayton was about to return the gesture when Levi's face changed, a flicker of horror running across it.

What the…?

A sound behind them had Clayton turning around, pulling Penny with him, almost knocking her off balance in his haste.

Mitch glared at them from down the barrel of a gun.

Penny screamed and covered her mouth, her walking stick dropping to the ground. He tightened his grip on her arm, pulling her in close, subtly trying to move her behind him.

"Thanks for bringing her right to me. You saved me the trouble of coming to find her." The man gave Clayton a mirthless grin that looked more ghoulish than anything else. Shit. Shit. Shit. What should he do?

"Come on, honey, you're coming with me." Mitch held out a hand to Penny, who flinched backward.

Mitch looked like he hadn't slept in days. His clothes were the same ones he'd been wearing the other morning, except they were crumpled and disheveled, his face drawn and pinched. So much for the sheriff's office saying this guy wouldn't be a problem. Clayton glanced around, looking for something he could use to fend off Penny's ex-husband off with.

"And don't either of you think about being a hero," Mitch called over Clayton's shoulder. He couldn't see Levi or Dale behind him, but by the look on Mitch's face, they must've been making a move toward them. "If you come any closer, I'll kill her."

Clayton's chest tightened painfully. Would he honestly do that? Take Penny's life, rather than let anyone else have her?

"Stop moving," he warned again. "If you even twitch another finger, I'll shoot. I mean it. Get your hand away from your phone."

Even while Mitch's concentration was on the two men farther down the parking lot, the gun never wavered from where it was pointed, directly at Penny's chest. The way he held the gun told Clayton he knew what he was doing.

Clayton quietly tried to maneuver Penny farther behind

him, sheltering her with his body. She'd gone terribly still, almost as if the sight of Mitch had paralyzed her.

"Stop it," Mitch barked, his gaze zeroing in on Clayton. "If you don't get out of the way, I'll shoot you and then shoot her. You'll lose either way, lover boy."

Clayton froze. This feeling of powerlessness wasn't new to him; he'd had the same sense of impotence after he'd been arrested for arson. But it didn't mean he had to like it.

"Right, Penny, let go of lover boy and come over here." Mitch's tone lost some of its menace and took on a hint of appeal. Did he genuinely think he was going to win her over? That she was going with him willingly? That his idea of a sham marriage was ever going to work?

Clayton kept his voice low and deadly serious. "No. She's not going anywhere—"

"Don't use that old cliché on me. Because it *will* be over your dead body if you keep interfering," Mitch warned.

Penny suddenly loosened her grip on Clayton's hand; pushed past him. "Don't hurt him, Mitch, I'll come with you."

"No, you won't." Clayton lunged, grabbing her arm. The gun went off. He flinched, expecting pain to spear through his body, but Mitch had only fired a warning shot over his head.

"Yes, she is. Because she knows what's good for her." Mitch reached for Penny, a sly grin edging over his face, even as he kept the gun trained at Clayton's head.

"Please, Clayton." Her blue eyes implored him. "I'll go with him." Then she turned around and walked away.

She was giving herself up to save him.

He stood impotently by as Mitch backed toward a nearby car in the parking lot, keeping an eagle eye on all three men, while Penny limped along beside him.

Clayton looked helplessly between Mitch and his gun and

the other two men, also standing, stricken, as they watched this asshole abduct Penny. He had to do something. He couldn't let him get away with this.

"You won't get far," he called. "The cops will set up roadblocks. They'll stop you before you even get out of the county." Clayton had no idea if this was true, but he wanted to spook the man. Make him second-guess himself.

Penny seemed to act on autopilot, she did everything he told her, sitting in the driver's seat while he secured her seatbelt, staring straight ahead through the windshield, eyes blank.

"Don't try and come after me," Mitch called over the roof of the car, as he got into the passenger side. "I mean what I said, I'll kill her if you do."

Clayton glanced back, Levi was on his phone, hopefully calling the police. Dale stood next to Star, his tanned face as pale as a ghost.

The car pulled slowly out of the parking lot, raising a plume of dust as it trundled down the dirt driveway.

Clayton couldn't stand here and do nothing.

People began to emerge from the path into the parking lot, confused concern on their faces as the sound of the gunshot drew them out. He ignored them; they couldn't help him now.

He glanced at Dale and Levi again, looking for inspiration.

Star let out a loud whinny, as if he knew how dire the situation was.

Clayton stared at the horse.

Then he was running down the grassy verge. He grabbed the reins and vaulted into the saddle before Dale could react.

"Yah." He rammed his heels into the chestnut's sides and leaned low over the pommel as the horse flew in a full gallop after the car.

He couldn't let that bastard take her.

CHAPTER SEVENTEEN

Penny drove slowly, but steadily down the familiar driveway. How many times had she driven this over the past two years? Too many to remember, but none of them had been with a gun held to her side.

Mitch sat in the passenger seat, smiling blithely at her, looking for all the world as if this were an everyday occurrence and they were back to being a married couple, as if none of the past two years had happened. Except for the gun he pushed hard into her waist. And except for how he kept checking the side mirror, to make sure they weren't being followed. This man next to her was a very different Mitch to the one she'd married. This man was a stranger. A deadly stranger. What was Mitch capable of? He said he would kill her, rather than see her go free. Her palms went cold and clammy at the thought.

She had no choice but to go with Mitch. Otherwise, he would've shot Clayton, and she couldn't let that happen. Because Clayton meant too much to her.

"I forgot to tell you how lovely you look today," Mitch said, leaning closer to her ear. "Even more beautiful than on the day we met."

Penny thought she might vomit.

"You should keep your hair blonde. I like it. Everyone back at home is going to love it."

Penny gave him a sideways glance. Mitch was completely delusional. How did he ever think that any of this was going back to the way it was before?

"Drive faster. You're going too slow. We've got a long way to go if we're going to make it home tonight."

Yes, she had been driving slowly on purpose. Waiting for what, she wasn't sure. Waiting for inspiration to hit as to how she could overpower her ex-husband and escape his clutches, perhaps. Or waiting for someone to come and rescue her.

"Faster," he demanded, and she flinched as he pushed the gun harder into her stomach. She planted her foot on the gas pedal and the car sprang forward. This part of the road was gravel; it turned to asphalt once they got to the highway. It also was quite winding, with a couple of sharp turns coming up to avoid two large trees. Pastureland followed them on the left, with native pine forest on the right. Even someone who'd driven this road a lot had to be careful.

Mitch stared into the side mirror. "What the fuck?" he said to himself. "Go faster," he shouted. She was already going as fast as she dared, but she pushed harder on the accelerator.

There was a flash of something in the rearview mirror. A blur of chestnut. It was a horse, thundering after them down the road. Her heart lodged in her throat. Who was it?

Mitch turned in his seat to stare through the rear window. "Who the fuck…? It's got to be lover boy, doesn't it?" Mitch laughed. "Is he crazy? What does he think he's going to achieve by riding after you like a knight in shining armor?"

Penny was thinking the same thing. It was extremely brave of Clayton—if it was Clayton on the horse—but how did he think a horse was going to overtake a car?

She couldn't shake the stupid feeling of elation, however. Clayton was coming for her. It was an unwise, unplanned, reckless thing to do. But he wasn't going to let her go that easily. The idea had her heart soaring in circles in her chest.

Then reality hit. Oh God, what if he tried something silly, like leaping onto the car windshield? He'd end up breaking his neck, or Mitch would shoot him, and either way he'd be dead. Penny increased the car's speed. She couldn't let Clayton catch up to them. She had to stay ahead. Once they got to the highway, he'd never catch them on a horse.

"Good girl, keep away from that crazy bastard." Mitch probably misunderstood her motivation for staying in front of Clayton, but at least he wasn't arguing about how fast she was going. And he'd withdrawn the gun from her stomach, although now he was waving it wildly in the direction of the galloping horse.

Even though she was now speeding along the gravel road as fast as she dared, the horse was gaining on them. There was a sharp curve coming up; she'd need to slow down for it.

She hit the brakes at the last second, slowing just enough to get the car around the corner, although it slid sideways a little. Mitch didn't seem to notice; he had his eyes glued on Clayton. The horse caught up when she slowed and had galloped alongside for a few moments. She could hear the sound of its hooves pounding on the dirt next to the car clearly. Then the horse was gone.

As she came out of the corner, Penny planted her foot again. She didn't need Mitch to urge her to go faster; she was desperate to stay ahead of Clayton.

But the horse flashed across the road, right in front of her.

She stamped both feet on the brakes in a last-ditch effort not to hit him. The wheels hadn't completely straightened after taking the corner, and the car's momentum swung the rear end around, putting it into a slide.

Mitch yelled something unintelligible. Then he grabbed the steering wheel, wrenching it away from Penny's grip, overcorrecting the car's course.

It was the wrong thing to do.

The car skidded off the gravel road, slewing sideways, the wheels spinning uselessly. There was a sickening crunch as the rear bumper hit a tree, spinning them into a half-turn, and then the car was careening straight toward an enormous, old, pine tree.

It was in that split second that Penny remembered Mitch didn't have his seatbelt on.

* * *

Clayton hauled on the reins and Star propped to a stop, his haunches nearly hitting the ground in his haste. Clayton leaped off into the grass before the horse had come to a complete halt. Fuck, the car had smashed into the tree. Steam hissed from the shattered engine and something was making ticking noises, but otherwise there was dead silence.

Was that his fault? He hadn't been thinking, only trying to stop the car with his mad dash in front as it slowed to take the corner.

Penny!

Was she hurt?

He took one step toward the car and there was a flash, then a loud explosion.

Star reared in fright and took off, back toward the lodge.

The engine was on fire.

Clayton ran, cursing the tight suit. It might've looked good when he was merely standing around, but the stupid thing was hampering his movement. Penny had been driving, so he made his way to that side of the vehicle. He opened the door to find Penny slumped over the steering wheel. White powder drifted around the cab and the remains of the airbag were floating over the dashboard. Mitch was... He didn't look good. He was slumped against the door and there was a huge gash on the front of his head. Blood covered his face, ran down his chin and onto his chest. It looked like, even with the airbag, he'd hit the windshield. Glass was shattered all around him.

"Penny. Are you okay? Wake up." He shook her shoulder, keeping one eye on the growing engine fire. She stirred and mumbled something, but didn't wake fully. Thank the Lord. She was alive. He reached around and unclasped her seatbelt, then tried to lift her out. Shit, her legs were trapped by the crumpled dash. Getting down on his knees in the dirt, he ducked his head under the dash. A jagged piece of plastic trapped one of her feet.

He stood up. How was he going to get her out? Flames licked higher, scorching the bark on the old tree, mesmerizing him for a second. Enough heat was emanating now that he almost had to hold his hand in front of his face to deflect it.

Of course. He bent down once more and released the latch beneath the seat, sending her backward. Thank God for Penny's short legs. By pushing the seat back as far as it would go, he garnered enough room to free her foot. He tugged her out of the car and lifted her into his arms.

"Clayton, is that you?" She opened one eye as her head lolled back in his arms.

"Yes, sweetheart. You're safe now. I've got you." There was a nasty bruise on her chin, and one eye was swollen shut—perhaps an injury from the airbag. He'd have to wait until he got her safely away from the car to check for other injuries.

Clayton carried her up the road to a stand of larch trees and put her gently down in the grass. Far enough away if anything happened. Should he go back for Mitch? That bastard didn't deserve to be saved, but he couldn't in all good conscience let him roast alive in a burning car. He'd better hurry, those flames were spreading fast.

"I crashed the car," Penny said, still a little groggy.

"I know," Clayton said, smoothing her mussed hair away

from her face.

"Oh." She tried to sit up straighter. "Mitch. Mitch was in the car, too." She swung her head around, as if looking for him. At least she seemed fairly unharmed, no broken bones. She could still have internal injuries, however. "We need to go and help him." Penny went to stand, and he put a hand on her shoulder.

"It's okay, I'll get him. You stay here."

"Thank you." She sank back against the tree trunk. Why in hell she'd want to save him, he had no idea. But she was right. He stood and turned to go back.

The tree where the car had embedded itself was now ablaze, the flames climbing into the lower branches. And the whole front of the car was alight. Not good. Clayton sprinted down the road.

Another explosion shattered the peaceful summer day, the force of it throwing Clayton backward.

By the time Clayton picked himself off the ground, he knew there was nothing he could do. The car was a burning ball of heat and flames. There was no way Mitch was coming out of there alive, if he'd actually survived the crash.

Clayton jogged back to where he'd left Penny. She was standing, holding onto the tree for support. Her face was ashen and her eyes wide. He enfolded her in his arms, hoping to shield her from the terrible sight.

A dozen cars sped over the hill behind them. People spilled out of the vehicles, all talking at once. Some of them ran to the flaming car, but backed away when they got too close, coming to the same conclusion Clayton had. There was no saving Mitch now.

Dean got out of his silver pickup with a fire extinguisher and tried to put out the fire.

Levi and Wyatt got out of another truck and Clayton heard Levi shout, "Call the fire department."

"He yanked the steering wheel. There was nothing I could do. I didn't mean to crash." Penny's voice was small, swallowed up by the folds of his dress shirt.

"I know, sweetheart." He hugged her tighter, running a hand through her hair.

"I didn't mean to kill him," she murmured. "I only wanted to live my own life."

CHAPTER EIGHTEEN

The soothing music of a string quartet playing softly in the corner of the glade was shattered by the sound of a motorcycle engine. Penny stood up straighter, casting a quick smile at Emily and Stella, standing beside her near the makeshift altar. She'd discarded the cane and was standing on her own, her ankle feeling better today. The wedding had been put off yesterday, after… Penny still struggled to think about everything that'd happened. But everyone concerned was determined it would go ahead today. Penny was more than happy to go along with the new agenda—she'd been devastated that she'd been responsible for the debacle that saw the wedding postponed.

Her hand fluttered up to touch the side of her face and she quickly lowered it again. There wasn't enough makeup in the world to cover her black eye, and she was feeling more than a little self-conscious about it. Clayton had told her not to worry, that she was beautiful in his eyes, no matter what. A hot stab of guilt pierced through her chest. Nope, she'd promised herself she wasn't going there today. Mitch was dead. She'd had a hand in his death. Yesterday had been terrible, and she still hadn't had time to process it. But today was all about Cat and Levi. She steeled herself, took a deep breath, and forced away the tears. Tomorrow, she would break down. Right in this moment, she would be strong.

The weather yesterday had been picture-postcard perfect; the most flawless day for a wedding. Today, however, there were purplish clouds hovering over the top of the Bitterroot Mountains, threatening a summer downpour. And the heat. It was hot today, much hotter than any day Penny could remember since she'd been in Montana. Almost as if the low clouds were trapping the heat in, and everyone was simmering in their own humidity. Most of the guests were fanning themselves with whatever came to hand as they sat and waited for the bride to make her way down the aisle.

Penny lifted her head to watch Cat ride slowly down the aisle, formed by rows of chairs on either side, on her Triumph. She was a picture of contradictory themes. The simple white dress—sleek and figure-hugging to show off Cat's willowy figure—and her spiked, blonde hair, so white it was almost silver—was at such odds with the big, black motorcycle. But it didn't matter, because it was so much the heart of who Cat was, that it made perfect sense to everyone standing here today. The simple, strapless dress did nothing to hide Cat's tattoos; if anything, it highlighted them. And again, this was how Cat wanted it. She'd never hide who or what she was. She deserved this wedding; deserved to be happy forever with Levi.

The enormous smile on Cat's face as she approached Levi said it all. A tiny, diamanté headband sparkled in her short hair, catching glimpses of the sun as it speared down through the gathering clouds.

Levi stood at the end of the aisle in his tuxedo, shoulders back, raven hair slicked back into a tidy man bun, an irrepressible grin on his face. He'd given away the idea of arriving on a horse. After the whole disaster of Clayton riding off on Star yesterday, he decided it might be better to leave the horse out of the equation today. His older brother Wyatt stood next to him, looking nearly as happy as Levi. Wyatt was slightly taller, clean-shaven next to his brother's beard—which was neatly trimmed and sculpted for the wedding, of course. Big Tom was Levi's other groomsman, and he, too, looked sharp and stylish in his black tux. Holy cow, they must be hot in those suits. She was sweating in her little strappy dress. Penny noticed a trickle of sweat run down Tom's temple, which he swiped surreptitiously away. But Levi seemed impervious to it all.

Her gaze found Clayton standing at the side of the crowd, and he winked at her. She hadn't allowed him to hide away up the back like he intended and told him if he tried to lurk down there, she'd march right down and drag him out, so he was front and center. He'd earned his right to be here, just like everyone else. She pressed her lips tightly together for a second. If only Clayton could've been the third groomsman, then everything would be absolutely perfect. But she understood that was impossible. Even after everything he'd done to save her, both after Mitch tried to abduct her the first time and yesterday when he chased down the car, people were still coming to terms with the fact he was a good man, after all. She'd known it all along. But as long as everyone else was beginning to realize it now, that was all she could ask for.

Penny caught sight of Jude, sitting in the back row with Sheriff Buchanan and Deputy Nomad. He'd been released from hospital yesterday and Penny was delighted to hear he could walk out under his own steam, albeit with a walking stick to help him stay upright. Perhaps the silver lining to this whole rescheduled wedding was that he was able to attend today. Penny needed to talk to him. He deserved her heartfelt thanks for what he'd done for her and Clayton. And she wasn't sure how she was ever going to repay him.

A low grumble overhead momentarily took her focus away from the motorcycle slowly approaching. She prayed it wouldn't rain.

Cat leaned the motorcycle onto its kickstand at the edge of the gathering and then skipped over to where Levi was waiting for her, hands outstretched. It was a pity Cat's father wasn't here to give her away. It'd been Cat's decision not to invite him. She would go and see him soon. She'd said it was better that way. Penny knew little of Cat's early life, and it was Emily who told her that Cat's dad was an alcoholic and he would never have coped with all these people; it would've all been too much for him. Which Penny thought was a touch sad. But Cat was more than happy to walk herself down the aisle, like the competent, independent woman she was.

The last ray of the sunlight disappeared, overtaken by gray clouds. But it remained stiflingly hot.

"Welcome friends and family," the celebrant began, and the few whispers and mutterings died down as he spoke. "We are gathered here today to join Levi and Cat together in matrimony."

The celebrant went on with the ceremony, but Penny tuned him out, instead watching Clayton's face out of the corner of her eye. That little furrow was back between his eyes. She was learning that it appeared not only when he was worried. It also materialized when he was deep in concentration or focused intently on something. And he was staring at Cat and Levi so earnestly, she wondered what he was thinking. Then his gaze flicked to her face, and it was almost as if she could read his mind. He wanted what they had. His eyes told her how much he hoped that could be him one day. Him and her, standing at the altar.

There was love in his gaze. Love for her. In that second, she knew. She wanted Clayton. Wanted to be with him. Penny had never believed in soul mates; that one person you were supposed to spend the rest of your life with, to be bound body and mind. Her time with Mitch had strangled any thoughts of magical love she might once have entertained. Mitch had proved to her that love could be dangerous and convoluted.

With Clayton, however… It was different. The moment they'd met, a spark had ignited inside her.

Perhaps soul mates did exist, after all. And if they did, then Clayton was hers. What else could explain this instantaneous attraction, this force so powerful it overrode all logic and coherent thought? What else explained why her heart beat faster whenever she looked at him? The feeling of safety and surety that overwhelmed her when those ice-blue eyes fixed on her, and only her.

Looking at him, she was lost in the depths of her surprising revelation. She was in love with Clayton.

The spell was broken when Emily moved next to her, swiping at a tear. What had she missed? She turned back just as Levi uttered his vows, which meant Cat had already spoken hers. Damn, she needed to stop daydreaming. Levi turned to face Cat, taking both her hands in his.

"Today, I marry my friend. The one I've learned from and shared with. I promise to respect the person you are, and I promise to keep our relationship exciting and alive. I promise to hold you with the tenderness and to have the patience that love demands. Today I marry the one I love."

There wasn't a dry eye in the clearing when Levi finished his vows, even as more thunder rumbled overhead.

"I now pronounce you husband and wife," the celebrant intoned.

Another clap of thunder sounded overhead, closer than the first.

"You may kiss your bride." The celebrant stepped back and let Cat and Levi have center stage. He took her face in both his hands and kissed her so sweetly Penny had to look away.

Then the rain started in a rush of big, wet drops, drenching the guests and wedding party alike before they had a chance to run for cover. Chairs were tipped over and people fled into the trees to find shelter from the pouring rain. The string quartet scurried to get their instruments protected from the rain.

Penny went toward Clayton, being jostled good naturedly by others all trying to take shelter. She looked back to Cat and Levi still standing at the altar in the clearing. Levi picked Cat up and whirled her around. She tipped her head backward, laughing up at the sky. They were so full of love for each other, even a cloudburst wouldn't ruin their day. Instead, they were embracing it. It was such a beautiful scene, a lump lodged in Penny's throat.

She wanted to be part of this. Taking Clayton's hand, she tugged gently. "Shall we join them?"

Clayton didn't hesitate. "Why not?" He led her out through the overturned chairs to the middle of the aisle and swept her up into his arms. Then they were dancing to the music in their heads.

Penny spied Stella and Wyatt huddling beneath the branches of a large fir. Stella grabbed Wyatt by the hand and dragged him into the clearing to join in. Then Tom and Emily were there, too. All of them hooting and twirling and stomping in the puddles like complete idiots.

The cloudburst was over almost as soon as it started. But it was long enough for them all to be soaked to the skin. The cooling rain had taken away the oppressive heat of the day and Penny felt refreshed and revived, even if her hair was now a tangled mess.

"That was the best wedding ever," Cat yelled, her crystal eyes flashing as she shook water from her hair like a dog.

They all congregated toward the bride and groom.

"You're not mad that the rain ruined your wedding?" Wyatt asked cautiously.

"Not at all," Cat replied. "I see it as a sign. We've been washed clean. A chance for a new beginning." As she said this, she stared straight at Clayton and then glanced at Penny. "What do you say? How about a new beginning?" She walked over and extended her hand to Clayton.

"That would be great," he said, taking her hand, not quite hiding the surprise in his face.

As Penny watched Cat finally forgive Clayton, she thought her heart might burst.

CHAPTER NINETEEN

Clayton took off his jacket and slung it over her shoulders. "Your dress is a little see-through after the rain," he said by way of explanation.

"It'll be okay once it dries." Penny giggled and snuggled into him. He let the feel of her sink into his core. She was amazing. If only he could find the words to tell her how he felt.

"Shall we all head up to the lodge?" Dean's voice rang out around the clearing. "We can do the witnessing of the signatures up there, don't you think?" His gaze found Cat amongst the small crowd and she nodded. It was a good idea, in case it rained again. Although, the clouds seemed to clear, almost as if that cloudburst had been it for the day.

The rest of the guests came out from beneath the shelter of the trees and filed their way up the path toward the lodge. After Penny checked with Cat that she didn't need her help—Cat only had eyes for Levi, and she waved all her bridesmaids away with a happy flick of her wrist—she came back to Clayton's side and they walked through the garden. The small amount of rain had refreshed everything, and green leaves sparkled with droplets, the damp earthy smell permeating the air.

"That was so cool," Penny murmured as she tucked in under his arm.

"What, dancing in the rain?" Who would've thought rain at a wedding could be a good thing? It'd certainly opened his eyes. But then everything in the past week had been a revelation to him. Things were looking up, finally.

"That too, but I meant what Cat did. Forgiving you, like that."

"Oh, yeah." It had been cool and unexpected. Clayton was more than happy to accept her forgiveness.

He glanced down at the woman snuggled beneath his arm. Her limp was still there, but her ankle seemed to be getting stronger every day. Clayton had noticed several times during the day, Penny's eyes glazed over, her face going sad and gaunt, as if she were lost in a memory. But she bravely pushed the obviously painful thoughts about her ex-husband away and smiled again. The bruising on her face and neck was still evident, even after she tried to cover it with layers of makeup. A solemn reminder of the past few days. But he'd hardly noticed it as he watched her standing beside Cat and the other bridesmaids. All he could see was how beautiful she was. The wedding thing had sparked something in his heart. Normally weddings left him feeling jaded and a touch cynical. Marriages never lasted; weddings were a waste of time, in his reckoning. This one had been different, however. Was it just that Penny was involved, and he was looking at it through fresh eyes?

They arrived at the area beneath the large wrap-around porch, which had been converted to accommodate the wedding reception. Clayton was briefly taken aback at what a superb job the Stargazer team had done to transform the area normally used for barbecues. Strings of fairy lights hung from the ceiling, and bunches of native flowers covered the tall pillars. The colors were black and white, with a few pastels thrown in to match the bridesmaids' dresses. Clayton was impressed. This wasn't your normal, froufrou wedding, full of frills and lace. He could almost appreciate the simple elegance of the whole thing.

Of course, in traditional Stargazer style, there was so much food, the tables were almost overflowing. Dean was nothing if not generous, and that generosity extended to always making sure people were well-fed. Joseph had outdone himself today. Clayton had heard via Penny that Joseph hadn't been happy when the wedding was postponed, but he'd salvaged a lot of the food and kept it for today. There was none of the fancy-pants food you might find at other weddings here. The tables were piled with Cat and Levi's favorite fare. Burgers, ribs, and barbecued meats. Potato salad, slaw and cornbread all filled the tables.

The centerpiece was the wedding cake, which Stella had made. It's simplicity matched the theme. Three tiers of plain white, with a spray of white flowers on the top and the words *Ride With Me Forever* written in black around the bottom tier. It wasn't until Clayton went right up close, he could see the flowers were actually handmade icing. They were so lifelike, Clayton hadn't been able to tell the difference. Stella sure was talented.

Penny hardly left his side, making sure he got a plate of food and hovering by him protectively, as if she still feared someone was going to say something upsetting to him. There were no designated tables, people stood around in groups and ate and chatted, or perched on strategically placed bales of hay and some old pine logs that'd been drawn up to act as seats. They joined Dale, Steph, Tom, and Emily in a small cluster. It took a while for Clayton to feel entirely comfortable, but when Tom turned to him and asked a question about one of the horses that'd gone lame, Clayton finally relaxed a little. He and Tom had been friends back before the fires. Clayton respected Big Tom, he had a steady persona and solid work ethic. It wasn't the easy banter he'd once been used to, but it was a start; the breaking down of barriers. Dale joined the conversation, and they were soon deep into the best way to treat a stone bruise in a horse, and Clayton was in his element, talking about horses again, with men who understood his passion.

Penny handed back his jacket after her dress dried, but he left it hanging over a chair. The cloudburst had freshened the air, but it was now hot and muggy again, as if they were in the tropics, not the middle of Montana. People came and went, drifting in for a chat, then moving on, but Penny stayed glued to his side. Eventually, even she was dragged away by Stella to help organize the knife for the cutting of the cake, and Clayton found himself alone for the first time that day.

"Great wedding." Dean suddenly materialized by Clayton's shoulder. He had a glass of champagne in his hand and he raised it in the air. "The venue is amazing. Even if I say so myself." He chuckled and Clayton thought that it might be the first time he'd ever seen his ex-boss a little tipsy. But who was he to judge? Dean deserved to be happy after all he'd been through in the past two years.

"Yes, it was great," Clayton agreed. "One of the best weddings I've been to."

"Hm." Dean's gaze suddenly zeroed in on Clayton. "And what you did yesterday was one of the best things I've ever seen. You were incredibly brave to go after Penny and that man in the car."

Clayton shook his head. "No, sir, it wasn't. I did the only thing I could think of. I couldn't let him take Penny away. It was reckless and irresponsible, and I wanted to apologize for taking Star like that—"

"Don't devalue what you did," Dean said quietly, but firmly. "I saw something in you yesterday that made me rethink everything I thought I knew about you."

Clayton was about to argue again, but something in Dean's face stopped him. "Well…ah, thank you, I guess." What did one say to your ex-boss, who'd mistrusted you so much he thought you were capable of trying to burn his lodge down, but who now seemed to be singing your praises instead?

"Did I mention that Dale, my nephew, is leaving soon? He's needed back at Stormcloud Station in Australia." Dean took a sip of champagne, his eyes never leaving Clayton's. "I'm going to need a new ranch hand to replace him." There was a pause and Clayton's skin prickled. "I was wondering if you wanted the job?"

Every muscle in Clayton's body tensed as if he were expecting a physical blow. Had he really heard Dean say that? Part of him didn't want to believe it. Because if Dean was pulling his leg, he wouldn't cope with the disappointment.

He stared at Dean, unable to form coherent words.

"Is that a yes, or a no?" Dean asked, one eyebrow raised quizzically.

"Yes, sir. I would be honored to take the job." How on earth he'd created lucid-sounding speech, he had no idea? Dean wanted him back? He was going to work at Stargazer again? It was almost incomprehensible.

"Great." Dean slapped him gently on the back. "I'll tell Naomi, she'll be pleased you're coming back. She always liked you." And with that, Dean flashed his genial grin and ambled away, shouting a greeting to one of the guests, then hugging him like a long-lost friend. Which he probably wasn't, Dean treated everyone with warm-hearted friendship. For a while Clayton had hated Dean for the way he'd treated him after the arson attacks, but now that veil of self-induced doubt he'd generated and saw Dean as he truly was. Dean had reacted to the crisis the way any other normal person would have.

Something brushed past his shoulder and Penny threw herself into his arms and kissed him. "I heard. I was standing behind you, but I didn't want to interrupt. Oh, Clayton, that's fantastic," she said, burying her face in his neck.

"Yes, it is." Clayton let himself smile wholeheartedly as the news sunk in. "And most of it is thanks to you."

"Holy cow, you can be dense sometimes." She whacked him lightly on the arm. "You deserve this, Clayton. Take this good thing and accept it, for once."

Clayton forgot where he was, forgot he was surrounded by wedding guests, and he kissed her. Drew her essence into his soul. She had overcome so much. She should be wary of all men. Yet, here she was, adoring him. She was breathtaking.

"I would like to ask you out. On our first official date. I want to take you to some fancy restaurant and show you off to the world."

"I think we're way beyond that now," she laughed, then her eyes lost their sparkle. "Are you sure you want to date me? After all that happened with Mitch, I mean? I'm a bit screwed up."

"We all have baggage," he countered quickly. "And if you're prepared to put up with mine, then I can certainly deal with yours."

She pursed her lips and considered him for a few moments. "True. Okay, if that's what you want, let's have a date." The wicked glint returned to her eyes, and she leaned in close. "As long as that date includes lots of sex back at your house afterwards." She whispered the words into his ear, so no one else would hear. His body was instantly on fire. That was unfair, coming on to him in the middle of a crowd. Because all he could think of now was taking her to his bed.

"Anything you want. My wish is your command," he said with a wink.

"What about tonight? Cat and Levi will leave to go on their

honeymoon soon, then I'm free."

Clayton couldn't believe his luck. He'd have to get rid of Harry, so they could have the house to themselves. Goddamn, he needed to think of something else fast, or Naomi was going to throw him off the property for lewd behavior. He pulled Penny in against him, to hide the evidence of his erection.

"Yes, yes, yes," he whispered hoarsely. "Now, can we talk about something else, before my new boss sacks me for being a sex-crazed degenerate, who can't keep his libido in check?"

She giggled at his discomfort.

"I like that I have this effect on you," she said, pressing her body surreptitiously closer.

"I like it too," he replied. "A lot."

They stared at each other, the rest of the world forgotten. The words were there, on the tip of his tongue. Was it too early to be falling in love with this woman? His eyes searched hers for the answer. Was six days long enough to know someone well enough to decide you wanted to spend the rest of your life with them? Because that was what he wanted.

"I know how you feel," she said, "because I feel it, too."

He let out a gust of air. It was as if she could read his mind. "We have something special," he agreed. "I'd like to see where it leads."

"Yes," she agreed.

The promise of what they would share tonight hung heavy in the air. He leaned in and touched his lips to hers. This had been one exceptional day. And she was one exceptional lady. He deepened the kiss, not caring anymore if people were watching. Against all odds, they'd found each other. And he was determined never to let her go.

EPILOGUE

The strike of the horse's hooves on the earth below sounded like a drumbeat in Clayton's heart. He couldn't help it, he let out a whoop of pure joy. This was the life. Galloping across an open, green pasture with nothing but the blue sky above.

Until finally, a fence line loomed, and he leaned back in the saddle and tweaked the reins. Thunder slowed to a canter and then a jog, the big palomino pricking his ears forward. Thunder had been his favorite horse, back when he'd first worked at the ranch. Clayton was glad to see his old buddy was as spirited and big-hearted as always.

He was going to be late for the lunchtime party if he didn't hurry. Checking on the mob in Selway's Pasture had taken longer than he expected. One of the heifers had gotten her head stuck in the fence. Cows were naturally curious creatures, and this one had obviously found something terribly interesting on the other side of the fence. It'd taken him fifteen minutes to free the animal, and the heifer hadn't made his job easy, struggling and mooing as if he were trying to murder her, not free her.

Clayton opened the homestead gate from atop the saddle and they were through and on their way toward the stable in seconds. The building was deserted when Clayton got there.

Damn, everyone must already be down at the lodge. It was Dale's last day here in Montana, and of course, Dean was throwing the biggest farewell party in his honor.

Clayton still felt like pinching himself sometimes, to make sure he really was working at Stargazers. The past three weeks had flown by. He'd handed in his notice at the building company. George said he'd be sad to see Clayton go, that he was one of the hardest workers he'd ever met. Clayton wasn't sad to see the back of the warehouse, however. Not that he was afraid of hard work, it just hadn't been the kind of work that lit him up inside. Being back on the ranch was his true passion.

Unsaddling Thunder, he gave the horse a quick rubdown and made sure there was feed and water in the stable before he strode out of the building toward the lodge.

The sound from the party hit him first. A loud gaggle of voices led him around the side of the lodge and to the undercover area. Clayton could hardly believe that a little over three weeks ago, this place had been decked out in all its finery for Cat and Levi's wedding. Now it was back to the rustic, utilitarian space more suited to a working cattle ranch.

His gaze zeroed in on Penny before he consciously looked for her. And it still felt like a blow to his chest in those first seconds when he spotted her. That little kick his heart gave every time he saw her face always managed to surprise him. Their connection felt as natural as breathing now. As if they'd been together for three years, not merely three weeks.

She was busy helping Stella serve the meat from the barbecue. He went up and slid his arm around her, placing a kiss on her cheek. "Hiya, gorgeous."

"Holy cow, you scared me," she said with a smile, placing a piece of steak on one of the guest's plates.

"I missed you," he whispered in her ear and was rewarded with the hint of a blush creeping up her neck.

But she whispered back, "I missed you too. Now go and help Tom with the drinks, will you?" She gave him a playful shove and sent him on his way. The bruising and injuries had all but disappeared from her neck and face. No more reminders of the past.

Clayton sauntered toward the table under the overhanging porch, where Tom was handing out drinks to the guests and staff. He'd meant what he said when he told Penny he missed her. It might sound sappy and went against his image of being a rough, tough cowboy, but he no longer cared. As he uttered the words, part of his mind had wandered to what might happen tonight, once they were alone again in their cabin. There hadn't been a lot of sleeping going on over the past week, that was for sure.

Clayton could still hardly believe that Dean had gifted Penny and him one of the couple's cabins to stay in. He wondered if perhaps Dean might be overcompensating a touch to make up for doubting Clayton before, but Penny told him not to be stupid, that he would give anyone the same chance. For the first two weeks after Clayton moved back to the ranch and into the single staff quarters, he and Penny had tried to keep their relationship as subtle as they could. But like most fledgling relationships, they struggled to keep their hands off each other. And every night, he would sneak into Penny's room—which she was lucky enough to have to herself since Stella had moved in with Wyatt—and try to be as quiet as possible. But clearly their attempts at being discreet weren't as good as they hoped. Steph, who wasn't one to keep her thoughts to herself, had blatantly told everyone listening that the reason she was so tired all the time was because she was being kept awake by all the *noises* going on in the room next door. Which made Penny blush bright red to the roots of her hair. Dale hadn't said anything directly, but he'd certainly slapped Clayton on the back and given him a knowing look.

Perhaps Steph or Dale got tired of their nocturnal exploits and had a word to Dean, or perhaps Naomi took pity on them and told Dean to add them to *our flock of young lovebirds*, as she liked to call them. Whatever it was, after only two weeks on the ranch, Dean asked them if they'd like to share a couple's cabin.

As part of the refurbishment of the ranch after the fires, Dean had built three extra cabins behind the single staff quarters, half-way up the hill, nestled beneath a stand of Douglas-fir trees. Tom and Emily shared the original, smaller cabin down near the lodge. Stella and Wyatt had been allocated the first of the three new cabins; they'd moved in around two weeks ago, once the new cabins were finished. Clayton and Penny had the second one. Who would fill the last one?

Cat and Levi were the other young couple on the ranch, and they were the only ones who lived in town, in Levi's rented house. Levi always said that his tame raccoon, Rekker, was the reason he stayed. But it also meant he was closer to his work at the ranger's office. If there was ever an emergency, it was that much quicker for him to get there from town.

Dean complained to Naomi that he was going to need to build three more staff cabins if this trend kept going. It'd become a bit of a running joke with the staff, that there were now more attached couples on the team than there were single members. Joseph liked to say there was something in the Stargazer water.

All Clayton knew was that life couldn't get more perfect.

He greeted Tom and began handing out sodas to the people queuing behind the table. The ranch was running at full capacity today, people enjoying their summer holidays, which were in full swing. Clayton and Steph were scheduled to take out a trail ride this afternoon with around twenty people, over to Lake Como for a cooling swim. He was looking forward to that more than he could say.

Dale stood with the small cluster of staff not currently helping with the party. Steph and Emily were there, sipping on a coke each, as were Violet and Joseph. Dale looked nervous, which was at odds with his normally laid-back and cheerful style. Perhaps he wasn't looking forward to going back to Australia as much as Dean said he was. Dale had been in Montana for over two years now, supposedly learning the tricks of the cattle trade before he went back to help his mother—Dean's sister—run the station over there. Then Clayton caught the longing look Dale cast in Violet's direction, and it all became crystal clear. Clayton had heard no rumors of the two of them getting together, so perhaps it was unrequited love. Whatever it was, Clayton felt sorry for the guy.

Dean appeared in front of their drinks table, and waved his hands in the air, hollering for quiet.

"Hello, everyone. Thank you for coming," Dean called, gesturing everyone to come in closer.

Dale ducked his head and moved to walk away, but Steph caught him by the arm and shook her head. Perhaps it had been this Dale was dreading all along. Dale was actually a shy guy, but he hid it underneath his cowboy bravado. He probably despised making a spectacle of himself.

Clayton slipped away from the drinks table, around the back of the crowd centered on Dean, and found Penny standing behind the barbecue. He pulled her in and nuzzled her hair. She smelled of all the things he loved, barbecued meat, a hint of smoke, the summer Montana air, and her fresh lemony shampoo.

Dean spoke again. "We're here today to wish my nephew safe travels back to his home country. For those of you who don't know, Dale has been with us on loan from my sister's property in Queensland, Australia. And now it's time for him to go back and take all his acquired knowledge and put it to work over there. Dale, come over here." Dean beckoned to his nephew and Dale grimaced but made his slow way through the gathered crowd.

Dean sang Dale's praises, while his nephew stood there, looking more than a little uncomfortable. Clayton noticed that a few of the female guests looked crestfallen. Dale was a handsome guy, and he never failed to attract the attention of the women. He never seemed to act on any of those infatuations, however, which Clayton had to give him credit for. He tuned out from Dean's speech, concentrating instead on the feel of Penny beneath his shoulder. She fit there perfectly, almost as if she'd been made only for him.

Penny nudged him and Clayton tuned back in just in time to hear Dean say something wholly surprising. "And we'd also like to welcome an old friend back to the ranch. If you've been out on the horses, you've probably already met Clayton Sabitino. He's replacing Dale and re-joined our team as one of our trusted cowboys." Dean pointed at Clayton.

Everyone turned to stare at Clayton. Penny drew back a little and smiled broadly at him, joining in the heartfelt applause.

He was back amongst friends and colleagues. A huge smile split his face. "It's great to be here, folks. Thanks to Dean and Naomi." He tipped his hat in their direction. The boss and his wife were standing hand in hand, watching with delight as everyone welcomed Clayton back into their hearts.

"And thanks to Penny." He scooped her up into an enormous bear-hug and she squealed. "I wouldn't be here without her." It was true, and it was time to tell her exactly how he felt.

"There's more food and drinks to be had," Dean shouted,

and everyone turned their attention back to him and away from Clayton and Penny. "Don't let this wonderful spread go to waste."

Clayton put Penny gently back on her feet but didn't let go of her. He sucked in a breath and his stomach did an odd somersault at the thought of what he was about to say. "I love you," he said gently. He hadn't said the words yet, because he was scared it was too soon. But he couldn't *not* say them anymore.

"Oh." Her lips formed the perfect O as she stared up at him. He almost laughed at the surprise on her face. But her features soon turned serious. What would her reply be? He'd turned every single scenario over and over in his head for weeks now until it almost drove him crazy. Was she about to reject him? Not say those three little words he desperately wanted to hear?

"I love you, too," she replied.

The air rushed out of his lungs. She loved him. Now, life was perfect.

*   *   *

Later that evening, after dinner service had ended, Penny made her way up to the cabin. Hers and Clayton's cabin. She could still hardly believe they had effectively moved in together after only three weeks. But her grandma used to say, *when it's right, it's right*, and Penny knew this thing with Clayton was about as right as anything got.

Clayton was waiting for her on the small front porch, seated in one of the brand-new Adirondack chairs, beer in hand. He stood up and took her into his arms. "How was the rest of your day?" Clayton kissed the top of her head and then leant back so he could look directly into her eyes.

"Good," she replied, meaning it. Today had been a good day. Dale's farewell had been a happy event. And then she'd been kept extra busy this afternoon, handling all kinds of guest requests. It was good to stay busy, it kept her mind off other things.

The unspoken tender meaning beneath Clayton's words was clear. Clayton was checking on her state of mind. He did it every day.

It was just under a month since Mitch had been killed and Penny was still coming to terms with his death. Which meant she had her bad days and her good days.

Clayton used lots of clues to keep a barometer on her mental health. He would pick up on little things she hardly realized she was doing. Like if she stared too long out the window without saying a word, he would touch her arm and bring her back to the present. Or if she started picking at her dinner, he would make a light joke about how terrible the food was at the ranch, to get her eating again. Or if he saw her rubbing her chest to try to rid herself of the pain that sometimes sat behind her breastbone, he would gently take her hand and hold it in his, kissing her fingers until she smiled. Sometimes it still shocked her to understand that this was what it was like to be in a healthy relationship. Clayton cared about her deeply, cared whether she was happy or sad. Mitch wouldn't have cared about her state of mind, all he cared about was whether she was doing things the way he wanted them done.

"I had a call from Bethany today," she said, moving past him to sit in the other chair, taking his beer from his hand and sipping the cold liquid.

"That's good." Clayton sat back down in his own chair, and she passed him back his beer. He reached over and took her hand, and they both tilted their heads back to stare at the sky.

"She's coming out for a visit next month. She wants to meet you."

"Oh." It was a simple reply, but there were all kinds of

loaded meanings in that one little word. Clayton still doubted himself. Even with all her assurances he wasn't the pariah he thought he was, he still struggled to believe people wouldn't think the worst of him.

"She's already partly in love with you, so don't worry. After I told her how you galloped after me on the horse to rescue me, she can't wait to meet you and thank you."

"Really?" She didn't need to turn her head to look at him to know he was rolling his eyes. He hated to be thought of as a hero and downplayed it anytime it was brought up. He kept saying he did what anyone else would've done in his place. Except Penny hadn't seen anyone else riding to her rescue that day.

"What about your parents, they're not coming too, are they?"

She laughed at the outright fear she heard in his voice. But she guessed meeting the parents-in-law was a big step in anyone's relationship.

"No, they're not," she assured him. "But I will go and visit them soon. My dad, especially, is worried about me." She didn't add that her mother was still a little dubious about what'd happened with Mitch, almost as if she didn't want to believe it. Because that would annoy Clayton no end. But Penny wasn't going to force the issue. If her mother chose not to believe her own daughter, then that was more her mother's issue than Penny's. She owed her parents a visit, however, after her two years of radio silence.

Clayton wasn't as easily swayed to go and see his family. He still held a grudge at the way they'd treated him when they thought he was guilty of arson. Penny would work with him, hopefully help him find forgiveness in his heart and try to mend the bridges between him and his father. There was plenty of time to do that. Because she was in this for the long haul, as was he. Right now, it was enough to be together.

Neither of them had mentioned it yet, but both of them knew they'd get married one day. Not that she needed marriage to cement a relationship.

And after her disastrous marriage to Mitch, Clayton understood how wary she was of re-entering that institution.

Her mind returned to Mitch. He'd been constantly in her thoughts.

She didn't miss Mitch. She'd more than moved on from their relationship in the two years she'd been at Stargazers, and she was definitely no longer in love with him. But, surprisingly, she was filled with grief over his death. Perhaps her part in the way he died made it worse. At night, bad dreams were a common occurrence, where she'd wake up screaming, trying to put out a fire she was sure was burning up the bed.

During the day, she would find tears running down her cheeks for no reason.

Through it all, her bright light in all of this sadness was Clayton. He kept her sane. He held her in his arms when she woke from a nightmare. He and her friends and her work at Stargazer Ranch were the solid ground beneath her feet. They would help her get through this.

"Did you hear from Jude yet?" Clayton shifted slightly in his chair, angling his body toward hers.

"Yes, he phoned this afternoon. He says the morgue is finally releasing the body. The sheriff is happy we can close the case now."

"That's great. Now we can finally put this to rest and get on with our lives."

"Hmm." Penny was a little more doubtful. These things tended to drag on forever. There were always more questions that needed a response, more paperwork to be filled out, more hours to be spent waiting for answers.

It was decided that Mitch's body would be shipped to

Montreal, where his parents now lived. His parents had contacted her two days after his death, demanding to know the truth of what'd happened to their son. Penny never had a lot to do with them. She and Mitch had only visited once during their whole marriage. The phone call with them had been torturous and draining. Of course, they didn't believe a single one of the charges aimed at Mitch; to them, he was their golden boy. And they accused her of all kinds of terrible things, including only marrying Mitch to get his money, which astonished Penny no end; Mitch wasn't rich, and she would never choose that kind of guy, anyway. In the end, Penny had hung up in tears, unwilling to listen to any more of their spiteful tirade. She understood they were hurting and perhaps, given time, they might start to see things in a different light. But she wasn't going to worry about it. She was over letting toxic people run her life.

There were other painful things that had to be sorted out, as well. Just the other day, Penny had been asked to go into the sheriff's office to identify some items found in an old barn which they thought might've belonged to Mitch. Clayton had gone with her for moral support. Penny recognized them and confirmed them as her ex-husband's. So now they knew where Mitch had been in those few days she and Clayton had been at the fishing shack and preparing for the wedding. He'd found a barn on a property near town and hidden out there, while everyone had assumed he'd gone home to Santa Barbara.

She was pleasantly surprised to find Jude back at work, but only on light desk duties, while his leg healed. He told them his rehab was going well, and he was walking without a stick. He was the one who took her through and showed her Mitch's items, a sweater and a set of notes in his handwriting, detailing all of Penny's movements over the past few months. It turned out he'd been stalking her for quite a while.

"We need to find Jude a girlfriend."

"What?" Clayton was taken by surprise at her change in topic. Penny had been astonished to learn Jude wasn't married; he didn't even have a girlfriend.

"Well, he's such a nice guy. Dependable, with a big heart. Not to mention, courageous and dedicated to his job," she added.

Clayton lifted an eyebrow but nodded his agreement.

"I might try and do a little matchmaking. Because everyone deserves to be as happy as you and me." She squeezed his hand, and he laughed.

"Give it a go. But I'm not sure there are many women in town that interest Jude. He's quite picky."

"I still want to try."

A companionable silence descended as Penny sorted through all the women she knew and tried to decide who would suit Jude.

"Cat and Levi are back from their honeymoon. They're coming to the ranch tomorrow to show us the photos of Hawaii. Naomi insisted." Penny giggled. She could just imagine Cat's face at having to sit through what she would consider the excruciating pain of talking about herself and showing photo after endless photo. But maybe Cat might've changed her tune. Perhaps she might enjoy showing off photos of her and Levi in love. Everyone was capable of change and acceptance when it came to love.

Thinking about Cat and Levi and how cute they were together, her thoughts turned to how much she loved Clayton. And how much she wanted to show him she cared. He'd finally declared his love for her today. She'd been holding off, waiting for him to make his own decision, even though she'd been ready to declare her devotion to him on the day of the wedding. She was so happy that Clayton was happy. He loved working on the ranch.

She stood up and moved around the front of his chair, lowering herself onto his lap, facing him and removing his Stetson, placing it on the little side table.

"Hey, cowboy," she murmured.

His face was lit by the single porch light above the door, and it cast interesting shadows over his features. His blue eyes pierced her with immediate heat. Two hands slid around her hips, holding her firmly in his lap.

"Yes, cowgirl," he murmured back.

"I'd like to take you inside now." She ran her hands gently over his square jaw, liking the feel of his two-day scruff beneath her fingers. She wriggled her hips seductively and felt Clayton's erection grow swiftly beneath her, as Clayton showed how much he liked that idea.

"Would you now?"

"Yes, I…" Her words were lost in his mouth, as she lowered her head and kissed him. It was slow and sensuous as she let her tongue slide across his lips, then dip inside his mouth. Her fingers curled into the short hair at the back of his neck. He tasted cool, like beer and summer night air. She could kiss him all night. Leaving his mouth, her lips slid down the side of his neck, nipping the muscle that ran down to his shoulder, then sucking it gently. His soft groan of pleasure had her legs going shaky with sudden wanting. Skin. She wanted to feel his skin. Wanted to run her fingers up and down his muscular abs and have him hiss with the sheer pleasure of her touch. Forgetting where she was, she let desire take control.

The button of his jeans was between her fingers and she was halfway to undoing it, when Clayton said, "I think it might be a good idea to go inside, before we give everyone on the ranch a show that they'll all remember." He stood in one swift movement, setting her deftly on her feet.

At least one of them was thinking clearly. She gave a girly

squeal and then giggled as he swept her up into his strong arms and carried her through the door. He was so sexy when he gave her what she wanted.

She fell more in love with him every day. Her very own courageous cowboy.

If you liked Cloudburst, then you might like the other books in the
Stargazer Ranch Mystery Series.

Combustion - Prequel Novella

Wildfire - Book 1

Firelight - Book 2

Snowbound: A Christmas Novella Book 3

Snowfall - Book 4

Also by Suzanne Cass
NEW
Stormcloud Station Series
(A Stargazer Spinoff Series)
Small Town Romantic Suspense
Clear Skies
Starlit Skies
Crystal Skies

Stargazer Ranch Romance Series
Small Town Romantic Suspense
Combustion: Prequel Novella
Wildfire
Firelight
Snowbound: A Christmas Novella
Snowfall
Cloudburst

Island Bound Series
Mystery Romance (on an Island)
Books can be read as stand-alone
Bound by Truth
Bound by Silence
Bound by the Stars

Colors of the Earth Series
Small Town Romantic Suspense
Books can be read as stand-alone
Shadows in the Dust
Shadows in Deep Blue
Shadows of Red Earth

Romantic Suspense
Single Title
Island Redemption

Glass Clouds
Chasing Bullets

Love in the Mountains Novella Series
Small Town Short Romance
Novellas can be read as stand-alone
Rain on a Tin Roof
Lost and Found
Rescue his Heart

Please Leave a Review

The greatest gift you could ever give an author is to leave a review. You will be helping other people to discover this book and making a difference to me as an Independently Published Author. If you liked this book and want other people to read it too, please leave a review.